## "Go Away!" Donna Cried. "I Don't Need You, And I Don't Want You. And Neither Does Louisa."

Heat rose up Jake's neck. "Dammit, woman! Did you ever stop to think that I might want to play a part in *my* daughter's life?"

Jake cupped the back of his daughter's tiny head. "You're dead wrong if you think she doesn't need me or want me." Trembling inside, as if his body had been hit by an earthquake, Jake lifted the whimpering baby up against his chest, patted her back and said, "It's all right, sugar baby. Daddy's got you now."

Donna looked up at the big man cradling Louisa against his chest, and for just a moment she couldn't breathe. The sight of father and child overwhelmed her senses. There was something essentially right about the two of them together. Strength protecting helplessness.

A powerful man guarding what was his....

Dear Reader,

This May we invite you to delve into six delicious new titles from Silhouette Desire!

We begin with the brand-new title you've been eagerly awaiting from the incomparable Ann Major. *Love Me True,* our May MAN OF THE MONTH, is a riveting reunion romance offering the high drama and glamour that are Ann's hallmarks.

The enjoyment continues in FORTUNE'S CHILDREN: THE BRIDES with *The Groom's Revenge* by Susan Crosby. A young working woman is swept off her feet by a wealthy CEO who's married her with more than love on his mind—he wants revenge on the father who never claimed her, Stuart Fortune. A "must read" for all you fans of Daphne Du Maurier's *Rebecca!*

Barbara McMahon's moving story *The Cowboy and the Virgin* portrays the awakening—both sensual and emotional—of an innocent young woman who falls for a ranching Romeo. But can she turn the tables and corral *him?* Beverly Barton's emotional miniseries 3 BABIES FOR 3 BROTHERS concludes with *Having His Baby.* Experience the birth of a father as well as a child when a rugged rancher is transformed by the discovery of his secret baby—and the influence of her pretty mom. Then, in her exotic SONS OF THE DESERT title, *The Solitary Sheikh,* Alexandra Sellers depicts a hard-hearted sheikh who finds happiness with his daughters' aristocratic tutor. And *The Billionaire's Secret Baby* by Carol Devine is a compelling marriage-of-convenience story.

Now more than ever, Silhouette Desire offers you the most passionate, powerful and provocative of sensual romances. Make yourself merry this May with all six Desire novels—and buy another set for your mom or a close friend for Mother's Day!

Enjoy!

Joan Marlow Golan
Senior Editor, Silhouette Desire

Please address questions and book requests to:
Silhouette Reader Service
U.S.: 3010 Walden Ave., P.O. Box 1325, Buffalo, NY 14269
Canadian: P.O. Box 609, Fort Erie, Ont. L2A 5X3

# HAVING HIS BABY
## BEVERLY BARTON

SILHOUETTE *Desire*®

Published by Silhouette Books

**America's Publisher of Contemporary Romance**

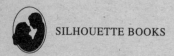 SILHOUETTE BOOKS

ISBN 0-373-76216-X

HAVING HIS BABY

Copyright © 1999 by Beverly Beaver

This edition published by arrangement with Harlequin Books S.A.

® and TM are trademarks of Harlequin Books S.A., used under license. Trademarks indicated with ® are registered in the United States Patent and Trademark Office, the Canadian Trade Marks Office and in other countries.

Look us up on-line at: http://www.romance.net

**Printed in U.S.A.**

---

## BEVERLY BARTON

has been in love with romance since her grandfather gave her an illustrated copy of *Beauty and the Beast.* An avid reader since childhood, she began writing at the age of nine and wrote short stories, poetry, plays and novels through high school and college. After marriage to her own "hero" and the births of her daughter and son, she chose to be a full-time homemaker, a.k.a. wife, mother, friend and volunteer.

When she returned to writing, she joined Romance Writers of America and helped found the Heart of Dixie chapter in Alabama. Since the release of her first Silhouette book in 1990, she has won the GRW Maggie Award and the National Readers' Choice Award and has been a RITA Award finalist. Beverly considers writing romance books a real labor of love. Her stories come straight from the heart, and she hopes that all the strong and varied emotions she invests in her books will be felt by everyone who reads them.

With love and gratitude to my husband, Billy, whose strength, kindness and understanding sustained me during some personally stressful months for our family, while I was writing this book.

# Prologue

"**I** can't believe I let you talk me into coming here." Donna Fields hissed the words under her breath as she glared at her friend, whose attention was focused on a group of rowdy cowboys at a nearby table.

"Admit the truth," Joanie Richardson said, her gaze riveted to one big, blond stud in particular. "You wanted to check this place out as much as I did. You've got to be tired of that lonely, boring existence you lead. I know I'm tired of being a Goody Two-shoes. Heck, gal, our vacation is almost over and I haven't had any fun yet. Let's live a little. Take a walk on the wild side, for a change."

Donna fumed as she glanced around the smoky interior of the Blue Bonnet Grill—a name highly inappropriate for the seedy establishment. Good sense had warned her not to give in to Joanie's fervent suggestion about spending their last night in New Mexico *out on the town*. For starters, there wasn't much of a town here in Plain City. In truth, it wasn't as large as their hometown of Marshallton, Tennessee.

"My life is neither lonely nor boring." Donna gasped when she noticed a couple in the far corner, their bodies pressed intimately together as the man devoured the woman's mouth. A warning shudder rippled over Donna's nerves. "Let's get out of this place. I feel uncomfortable in here."

Joanie glanced away from the blond roughneck, who was smiling at her, and followed Donna's line of vision to the couple in the dark corner. "Would you look at those two! I can't even remember what it feels like to be that passionate with a man."

"People shouldn't make public spectacles of themselves. It's disgusting!"

"You're just jealous."

"You're crazy."

"Those two are so caught up in the moment that everyone and everything has ceased to exist except the two of them." Joanie sighed dramatically. "I'd like some handsome guy to back me into a dark corner and—"

"Howdy, ma'am. My name's Big John." The blond giant stood beside their table, a wide smile on his face and a twinkle in his eyes. "Would you and your friend like to join me and a buddy of mine?"

"Yes, we'd love to," Joanie said.

"No!" Donna jerked on Joanie's arm. Leaning over, she whispered, "Have you lost your mind?"

"I'm just waiting around with some guys from the ranch until my buddy shows up. He should be here any minute. We could order us a round of beers and some big ole' steaks and have us a really good time."

"Sounds like a plan to me." Joanie scooted back her

chair and stood. She laced her arm through the cowboy's. "I'm ready for a good time."

"What about you, ma'am? My friend's an all right guy. I think you'd like him." Big John bestowed his devastating smile on Donna as he surveyed her from head to toe. "I know J.B. sure would like you. You're a bit classier than his usual type, but you've got the kind of looks that would interest him." Big John's gaze lingered on Donna's breasts.

Donna crossed her arms over her chest. The man's blatant perusal of her size 36-D chest bothered her greatly. Men could be such pigs. The only thing most of them had on their minds was sex.

Joanie mouthed the word *please* as she stared straight at Donna. "My girlfriend is a little shy. You can tell she's not the barroom type." Joanie repeated her silent plea to Donna, then turned her attention to Big John. "We're schoolteachers—actually we teach at a junior college in western Tennessee and we've been out here in New Mexico on an archaeological tour. Tonight's our last night."

"Then we should show you girls a good time before you leave."

When Donna just sat there, unmoving and silent, Joanie sighed in disgust, then cuddled up to Big John's side. "You and I can dance while we wait for your friend." She glanced at Donna. "Why don't you think things over while Big John and I are dancing? Please, honey, let's stay and have a good time. Do it for me."

Donna wanted to strangle Joanie. The two of them were more friendly acquaintances than true friends. They had met two years ago when Joanie was hired as a physical education instructor at the college where Donna was a history teacher. She liked Joanie, but she had very little in common with the woman, a twenty-eight-year-old recent divorcée. On the archaeology tour, they had been roommates and teammates. Joanie was good-natured and easy to be around—most of the time.

When Joanie had suggested having a little fun tonight, Donna had felt she couldn't refuse one simple request, even though she herself wasn't the type who was always looking for a good time. But the minute they entered the Blue Bonnet Grill, Donna had known she should have stayed at the inn.

The music was loud country hits blaring from an old jukebox. Smoke from countless cigarettes and cigars soiled the air a hazy gray. Men and women—mostly cowboys and barflies—shared beers, laughter, dances and kisses in dark corners. This was the last place on earth Donna Fields wanted to be. If her family could see her right now, they'd be appalled. She was, after all, a lady. Born and bred a blue-blooded, genuine Southern belle.

She glanced at the couple groping each other in the corner and felt a flush of heat rise up her neck and into her face. She wasn't by nature, a voyeur, so why couldn't she stop watching the man and woman? While she was in the middle of giving herself a good talking to, the man wrapped his arm around the woman's shoulders, led her across the smoke-filled room and out the front door, which was only a few feet from the table where Donna sat. An uncontrollable shiver rippled along her nerve endings. Instinctively, she knew the man and woman were headed for a motel room somewhere nearby. A tingling ache radiated up from the feminine core of her body at the thought of what the twosome would soon be doing.

Get your mind out of the gutter! she chastised herself. Then the more benevolent side of her personality pointed out that it was only natural for a healthy woman in her prime to think about sex, especially when she hadn't had any in five years. It wasn't that there hadn't been opportunities. She had dated several nice men who were eager to have an affair with her. But for her, sex meant a commitment. And commitment meant love. And love meant taking a chance on being hurt again. After she'd lost Edward, she swore she'd never love anyone again. Losing her husband had devastated her. She couldn't bear the thought of going through that kind of agony again.

Donna's misty-eyed gaze traveled around the room and rested on Joanie and Big John, whose bodies were welded together as they slow-danced to an old Hank Williams's tune.

Well, from the looks of that, she knew she'd be walking back to the Yellow Door Bed and Breakfast Inn by herself tonight. Joanie was definitely in heat. Tonight would be Big John's lucky night.

The outer door swung open and a gush of hot summertime air hit Donna full-force. She glanced up as several customers called out a greeting to the new arrival. Even the bartender threw up a hand, smiled and hollered a welcoming hello.

"Hey there, J.B.," the bartender said. "It's been mighty quiet around here without you."

Mighty quiet around here? Was the man kidding? If this place got any livelier, someone would have to call the police.

Suddenly Donna noticed the large, muscular man who had entered. The one called J.B. Big John's friend. This was the guy who was supposed to be her *date* for tonight? Not on your life. She had to get out of here—now!

Where Big John resembled a well-worn teddy bear and possessed a devastatingly sweet smile, J.B. resembled a black panther, his grin anything but sweet. There was an aura of danger around J.B. This man was no ordinary cowboy.

Big John stopped dancing long enough to wave at J.B. and call out to him from the small dance floor in front of the jukebox. "Hey there, man. About time you got here. Your girl's sitting right there at the table by the door. Buy her a beer, will you? Her name's—" He looked at Joanie.

"Her name's Donna," Joanie yelled. "Whatever you do, J.B., don't let her run out on you. She's a woman who needs to have a good time."

Donna wished the earth would open up and swallow her. Better yet, she wished the earth would open up and swallow everyone in the Blue Bonnet Grill, except her. She turned her back, hoping J.B. would take the hint and leave her alone.

The scrape of a chair being pulled out warned her that the rugged cowboy hadn't taken the hint. Maybe if she ignored him, he'd go away.

"Donna?" His voice had a hard, gravelly tone. Sand-paper rough. Baritone deep.

She nodded, then turned slowly and faced the most alarmingly attractive man she'd ever seen in her life. J.B. was a hunk. Pure and simple. But she was sure nothing about this man was either pure or simple.

He shoved the tan Stetson back on his head and a few strands of coal black hair fell down across his forehead. He stared at her with eyes so dark they appeared to be as black as his hair, but were actually a rich soil brown. His face, though handsome, was lean and hard. Not a pretty boy. And his dark, heavy beard stubble made him look as if he had a perpetual five o'clock shadow.

J.B. narrowed his gaze, focusing on her face, then he looked straight into her eyes.

Donna shivered involuntarily. The sexiest man alive was looking at her as if she were an item on the menu he was seriously considering ordering.

"Look, J.B., this date wasn't my idea," Donna told him. "My friend Joanie and your friend Big John—"

"What are you doing in a place like this, sugar? You're about as out of place here as I would be at the opera."

"I—I came with Joanie. This is our last night in New Mexico and she wanted to soak up some of the local night-life." Donna folded her trembling hands together and held them in her lap.

J.B. glanced over at the dance floor. "Where are y'all from—you and Joanie?"

He smiled at her then, a smile she was sure had lured many a woman to her ruin. A man like that probably had never heard the word no from a woman's lips.

"Tennessee," she said.

"Really. I used to live in Tennessee."

She didn't believe him, of course. If she'd said Alabama or Texas or Virginia, he'd have told her he used to live there. "Is that so?"

"Yep. Years ago." J.B. let his gaze travel leisurely from her face to her neck and then let it rest on her large breasts that even the loose-fitting purple blouse couldn't disguise. "How about a dance?"

"No, thanks."

"I promise I don't bite."

She glared at him suspiciously. He burst into laughter, then slapped the top of the table with his big hand. Donna jumped from the unexpected action. Their gazes met and held for an infinite moment. Her breath caught in her throat.

"What's the matter, J.B.?" a young cowpoke sitting at the next table called to him. "Don't tell me you've finally met a gal you can't sweet talk into the sack."

All the men at the young man's table exchanged a few crude comments, then laughed heartily. J.B. scowled at the baby-faced cowpoke.

"Maybe you're not her type." The man rose from his chair and walked over to Donna's side. "Is that it, honey bunch? You like your men younger and sweeter than ole' J.B.? If that's the case, then I'm your man."

"Leave the lady alone, Woody," J.B. warned.

"I ain't going nowhere until the lady tells me to." Woody leaned over, right in Donna's face, and placed a sweaty hand on her shoulder. "Why don't you join me and my friends? J.B.'s got enough women already. He don't need one more."

"Please." Donna wanted to scream and run away. She'd never been so embarrassed in her life.

"Honey bunch, I'd be more than glad to please you," Woody said.

Donna looked to Jake for help, her eyes pleading with him. "Please, go away and leave me alone. I—I'm J.B.'s date."

The moment she spoke the words, she wished them back. Why on earth had she committed herself to J.B.? She could have gotten herself out of this awkward situation some other way.

"You heard the lady," J.B. said. "She's mine."

Woody hesitated for a moment, but when J.B. stood, his big body towering over the smaller man, Woody grinned and stepped away from Donna. "Sure thing. I know better than to try to take something you done put your brand on."

Woody disappeared. The only thing Donna saw was J.B.'s long, lean legs, his broad shoulders and his smoldering dark eyes devouring her. He held out his hand.

"Let's dance," he said.

Reacting purely on feminine instinct, Donna rose, put her hand in his and allowed him to lead her over to the dance floor. The moment he took her into his arms, she knew she was lost. Lost to the most overwhelming sexual attraction

she had ever felt in her life. Lost to the seductive look in
J.B.'s eyes, the alluring heat of his hard body and the her
own long-suppressed desire.

How was it possible that she could want a man she'd
met only a few minutes ago? The thought was insane. She
was insane! But crazy or not, she wanted J.B. Wanted him
in a way she'd never wanted another man. It was as if some
wanton woman had taken possession of her body.

He pulled her closer as they began to sway to the music's
beat. His hold was undemanding and yet undeniably possessive. She didn't resist when he cupped her hip in one
hand and slipped the fingers of his other hand around her
neck.

"Lady, you're the sexiest thing I've ever seen." He
mouthed the low, breathy words against her ear.

She knew she was attractive, but she'd never thought of
herself as sexy. Feminine, yes. Sexy, no. Big breasts alone
didn't make a woman sexy, especially if she avoided dis-
playing that particular asset to full advantage. She was a
lady, and ladies weren't supposed to be sexy. Most of the
men she'd dated since Edward's death had considered her
an ice queen. A few had even told her she was frigid.

"J.B., I—I don't... I've never..."

He lowered his head. She saw his mouth coming toward
hers and knew what he was going to do. She could have
stopped him. But she didn't.

He kissed her. Hard and hot and hungry. Skyrockets exploded inside her. Everything female about her reacted to
all that was so very male about him.

This couldn't be happening. Not to her. Not to Donna
Deirdre Fields. She'd never been publicly affectionate with
a man. She had always considered public displays of emotion quite vulgar. But here she was, kissing a stranger, in
a seedy bar, in a one-horse town, in the wilds of New Mex-

ico. And she was enjoying it. No. More than enjoying. She was loving it.

He ended the kiss abruptly. She gazed up at him, knowing full well he could see the desire in her eyes. "We'd better stop, unless we want to put on a real show for the folks."

She nodded, then when he urged her head down onto his chest, she complied and cuddled against him. While their intimately entwined bodies moved slowly in a sensual dance, Donna listened to the thundering beat of J.B.'s heart.

One song ended and another began. Time stood still. She wasn't sure how long they danced. Had no idea what time it was. Didn't even know exactly when Joanie and Big John had left the dance floor, ordered steaks and eaten dinner. Everything and everyone outside the realm of J.B.'s embrace disappeared.

"I want you, sugar," he whispered. "I want you bad."

"I know." She felt his large, pulsating sex against her body as they danced.

"I'm staying in town for the weekend." He pressed his shaft against her mound. "I've got a room over at the Crescent Motel. Stay with me tonight."

"I—" It had been on the tip of her tongue to say no. To tell him that she wasn't the kind of woman who would spend a night at a motel with a man she barely knew. "It would be just for the night. After that, we'll never see each other again. Do you understand?"

"Just sex, sugar, that's all I want. Isn't that all you want?" He caressed her buttock, then cupped it.

Moisture flooded her body in preparation. She'd never ached so badly to have a man inside her. This hunger was unlike anything she'd ever known. "Yes, sex is all I want."

"Then let's go." He stopped, grabbed her hand and led

her off the dance floor. ''We need to tell your friend you're leaving with me.''

They paused momentarily at Joanie and Big John's table. The couple glanced up and smiled.

''We're heading out,'' J.B. said.

''Joanie, I, er, I'll see you in the morning.''

Joanie's big blue eyes rounded into surprised saucers. ''Oh! Uh... Yeah. Sure.'' Joanie smiled. ''Have a good time.''

In that one split second, Donna almost backed out. Almost. She knew what she was doing was crazy. The craziest thing she'd ever done in her life. But something inside her urged her on, encouraging her to sample forbidden fruit. To take a wild ride on an untamed stallion.

# One

The baby in her arms whimpered. Donna lifted Susan and Hank's son to her shoulder and crooned comforting, nonsensical words into the infant's ear. Sighing, she stretched her back, which ached unbearably. A symptom of late pregnancy and the fact that she had been on her feet too long today. But this was such a special event. A wedding. Susan Williams, one of her best friends, had married the man of her dreams, the only man she'd ever truly loved. The father of her child. Donna sighed as she watched the happy couple cut their wedding cake.

Just as Susan pushed a piece of cake into Hank Bishop's mouth, his sister Tallie cried out from the hallway, then burst into laughter.

"My God, Jake! I can't believe it's really you! After all these years you've come home," Tallie said. "You're too late for the wedding, but the reception just started."

"You don't mean our big brother actually came home

for your wedding," Caleb Bishop said. "Will wonders never cease. He didn't bother making the trip for Tallie's wedding or for mine."

"Well, this does make the day perfect, doesn't it?" Susan said. "All three Bishop brothers together for the first time in…how long?"

"Nearly eighteen years," Hank said, slipping his arm around Susan's waist as he led her over to meet the new arrival.

Donna Fields froze to the spot as she watched the Bishop family greet the tardy guest. They had called him Jake and had welcomed him as their long lost brother. But that couldn't be, Donna thought. It just wasn't possible!

Suddenly she felt light-headed. The room spun around and around. She couldn't faint. Not now. Not while she was holding little Lowell Bishop.

Donna called out to Danny Bishop, Caleb's twelve-year-old son. "Danny, will you take Lowell for a few minutes? I need to check on something in the kitchen."

"Sure thing, Miss Donna." The tall, lanky boy reached out and accepted the tiny bundle.

"Just take him over to your aunt Tallie if he puts up a fuss."

"Will do," Danny said.

Donna wanted to run. As fast and as far as her shaky legs would carry her. Unfortunately, she couldn't maneuver very fast in her present condition. She was as big as a barrel. Dr. Farr had told her that if she hadn't gone into labor by tomorrow, he intended to induce labor. She'd be so glad to get the birth over with and hold her precious little daughter in her arms.

Donna eased past several people gathered at the back of the dining room, smiling and nodding as she made her way toward the kitchen. She swung open the door, then closed it behind her and took a deep, calming breath. She had to get out of this house—away from the eldest Bishop brother! Dear God in heaven, why had he shown up today? Hank and Caleb's mysterious big brother had stayed away for more than seventeen years. No one thought he'd attend the wedding. But here he was—big as life and twice as dangerous.

Donna's heart raced so hard and fast that the drumming roared in her ears. Of all the men on earth, why him? Maybe she'd been hallucinating. Maybe she had imagined that Jake Bishop looked like J.B. After all, for the past nine months, ever since she'd said goodbye to J.B. at the airport, she had been unable to erase his memory from her mind. And when she had discovered that, despite the precautions they'd taken, she was pregnant with his child, the big, sexy cowboy had been on her mind constantly.

*Take another look at Jake Bishop and make sure he really is your J.B. from the Blue Bonnet Grill.* She eased the kitchen door ajar slightly and peered through the crack. The large, broad-shouldered man had his back to her. She quickly scanned his body from the top of his silky black hair to the heels of his snakeskin boots. He was the same height and size as J.B. Had the same coal black hair. The same dark complexion.

His deep, hearty laughter rumbled loudly. Donna's heart caught in her throat. Oh, God, she knew the sound of that laughter. The big man turned just enough to give her a glimpse of his face. The bottom dropped out of her stomach. This was no hallucination. No wild imaginings. Jake Bishop and J.B.—her weekend cowboy, the father of her child—were one and the same.

She couldn't let him see her. She had to leave before the two of them came face-to-face. But her purse and car keys were upstairs on Susan's bed. How could she slip upstairs without being seen? The house was filled with wedding guests. She'd just have to chance it. There was no other way. Besides, maybe, if she kept her head down and her face diverted, J.B. wouldn't recognize her. After all, the last time he'd seen her, she'd been thirty-five pounds lighter and actually had a waistline.

Another of those annoying back pains hit her the moment she walked through the kitchen door. She stopped abruptly, waiting for the pain to subside. As the last ripples of discomfort eased away, Donna took a deep breath, glanced quickly in J.B.'s direction, then jerked her head downward when she realized he was looking directly at her. As she made her way around the room, doing her best to avoid being noticed, a strange sensation came over her.

"Oh, God, no!" she pleaded under her breath just as her body betrayed her. Her water broke, sending what felt like a tidal wave down her legs and onto the floor. She stood there helpless and mortified.

"Oh, hell's toenails," Tallie shouted. "Donna's water just broke. Call Dr. Farr."

Within seconds, Tallie Bishop Rand, Susan Bishop and Sheila Bishop hovered around Donna. She prayed that their bodies protected her from J.B.'s curious stare. But within seconds, she realized that her prayer hadn't been answered.

"Donna?" J.B.'s voice boomed like thunder. "Donna, is that you?"

Jake moved across the room with deadly force, his eyes narrowed, his jaw tight. He parted the trio of Bishop ladies surrounding Donna and took a good look at the woman who stared back at him with amber cat eyes. It was her! *His* Donna from the Blue Bonnet Grill. The woman who had come to pieces in his arms time and again during that long weekend nine months ago. Nine months! He stared into Donna's pale face, then his gaze traveled downward to her large, protruding belly. She was pregnant. Very pregnant.

"What's the matter with you, Jake?" His sister Tallie tried to shove him out of the way. "Donna's water just broke. We need to get her to the hospital."

Jake didn't budge. "You're pregnant," he said to Donna. She didn't speak, only nodded agreement.

"Nine months' pregnant?" he asked, though the answer was more than obvious.

She nodded again.

"Will you get out of the way," Tallie scolded. "This has nothing to do with you. Just let us handle things."

"It's mine," Jake said, his deep, quiet voice silencing the chatter around the room.

Donna cringed as another pain sliced through her back. She gulped in air, then looked Jake square in the eye. "Yes" seemed to be the only word she could manage.

"What?" Tallie stared back and forth from her eldest brother to her pregnant friend.

Jake shoved the women aside and lifted Donna, whose damp dress clung to the backs of her legs. She slipped her arm around his neck and laid her weary head on his shoulder.

"I took a cab from the airport," Jake said. "Somebody else will have to drive us to the hospital." He carried Donna through the midst of curious onlookers, straight to the front door and out onto the porch.

His brothers and their wives followed, whispering among themselves as they tried to make sense of what was happening.

"We can take my minivan," Susan said, turning to her husband. "Get the keys and bring Lowell with you. He'll be hungry soon."

When Hank returned to the house to retrieve the keys

and his infant son, Caleb laid his hand on Jake's shoulder, halting Jake's progress toward the driveway.

"Mind telling us just what's going on here?" Caleb asked. "We're all a bit confused."

Jake paused, turned his dark gaze on his youngest brother and grunted. "You think you're confused! How the hell do you think I feel, showing up for Hank's wedding and running into a woman I spent a—"

Donna cried out in pain. "Please, hurry up and get me to the hospital. I'm sure I'm in labor and this baby isn't going to wait around while we discuss who's confused and why."

Caleb's wife Sheila slid open the minivan door. Jake stepped up inside the vehicle and settled Donna on his lap. She squirmed against him in an effort to remove herself from his arms. He tightened his hold on her just enough to restrict her movements.

Lowering his head so that his words were a whispered question in her ear, he said, "How about explaining a few things to me?"

"What's there to explain?" Tilting her chin defiantly, she glared at him as she shrugged her shoulders.

Jake stared meaningfully down at her stomach. "That baby's definitely mine, right?"

She tried again to wiggle free of his hold, but to no avail. "The baby is mine!" she told him. "I didn't think I'd ever see you again. I had no idea you were Jake Bishop. If I'd known, I never would have—" She lowered her voice. "You do realize, of course, that your showing up here like this has complicated my life. I told people that I had married and gotten a quick divorce and the father of my child was out of my life."

"Why didn't you get in touch with me to let me know I was going to be a father?"

"How was I suppose to do that? I didn't even know your last name."

"You could have—"

"Excuse us," Caleb said as he helped Sheila and Susan, who was carrying little Lowell, up into the van. "We're ready to go now."

Tallie raced toward the van with her husband Peyton at her side just as Hank opened the driver's door. She stuck her head inside, peered into the back and said, "Peyt and I will follow y'all to the hospital. And before Donna has her baby, this family expects a full explanation from you." She pointed her finger directly into Jake's face.

Donna groaned as another pain hit her. This had to be some horrible nightmare, she thought. It wasn't possible that she was on the verge of giving birth to Jake Bishop's baby. The child she had carried for nine months was hers and hers alone. Not once had she ever considered the possibility that her child's father would show up unexpectedly in her life. And it certainly hadn't crossed her mind that the man she'd spent the weekend with in New Mexico was the brother and brother-in-law of her three closest friends.

She had heard them mention Jake Bishop, the eldest of the Bishop clan, the brother who had left town nearly eighteen years ago and hadn't been heard from until about six years ago. In all that time, nothing had lured him home. Not his grandfather's death, not his other siblings' marriages, not even Caleb's nearly fatal accident. So, why now, after all this time, had he decided to show up for Hank and Susan's wedding?

Donna felt decidedly uncomfortable cradled in Jake's lap, but he'd made it abundantly clear that he wasn't letting go of her. She stole a glance at his face, hoping to gage his mood. But that stony, expressionless face gave away nothing.

"J.B.—ah, I mean Jake—" She cleared her throat. "—Why did you come back to Crooked Oak?"

"Yeah, why did you come back?" Caleb asked as he turned halfway around in the front seat.

"I came back for Hank's wedding," Jake said.

"Why for Hank's and not for mine or Tallie's?" Caleb draped his arm across the seat as he focused his gaze on his eldest brother.

"Well, to be honest, I was planning on coming back to Tennessee anyway," Jake admitted. "You see, I've made an offer for Old Man Henry's quarter horse ranch and if the deal goes through, then I'm moving home to stay."

"Well, I'll be damned." Hank slammed his hand down on the steering wheel. "Looks like, one by one, all three Bishop brothers have come home to roost."

Donna moaned. Oh, great! Jake Bishop was moving back to Tennessee. He'd be around all the time. She didn't think she could bear having him in the same state, let alone the same county. What if he wanted to play a role in little Louisa Christine's life? She barely knew him but somehow she was sure this cowboy wasn't suitable father material.

*You should have thought of that before you slept with him,* an inner voice chastised her.

"So, while we're on our way to the hospital, how about one of you explaining the situation to us," Sheila said. "It's obvious that you two know each other and that…well, are we wrong to assume that Jake is the father of your baby?"

"I thought you told us you didn't know the guy you spent the weekend with," Susan said as she rocked a restless little Lowell in her arms.

"I didn't know him!" Donna said. "All I knew was that his friends called him J.B. I had no idea he was Jake Bishop."

Caleb chuckled, then rubbed his chin in mock seriousness. "Let me get this straight. Donna and Jake met…somewhere…nine months ago, got married, got divorced and never knew who the other one was? Sorry, folks, but that doesn't make any sense."

"We didn't get married." Donna looked pleadingly at Jake.

"Oh, so you just had sex and then went your separate ways and Donna made up the story about a marriage and a divorce," Hank said.

"He wasn't suppose to show up in my life," Donna explained. "Not ever. J.B. was just a weekend fling. I had no idea I'd accidently get pregnant."

"So you did use condoms?" Caleb barely suppressed a grin as he looked his eldest brother square in the eye.

"This conversation is getting entirely too personal," Donna told them, then cried out when another labor pain struck.

"How far is the damn hospital?" Jake ran a comforting hand over Donna's stomach.

"We'll be there any minute," Hank said.

Donna clutched Jake's strong hand and held on to it tightly as the pain worsened and then subsided. Her cry transformed into a whimper and then a sigh of relief.

"Is it bad, sugar?" Jake asked, sincere concern evident in his dark eyes as he stared at her face.

"You have no idea." For a split second Donna was glad her baby's father was with her, holding her, comforting her, trying his best to reassure her. But the moment ended quickly and reality set in. She didn't know this man—Jake Bishop—and had no idea what his presence in her life would mean to her and her child.

"We're here," Hank said as he pulled the van up in front of the emergency room entrance.

Caleb jumped out, opened the back door and moved out

of the way as Jake emerged with Donna in his arms. Jake stormed into the ER, past the protesting receptionist and straight toward the nearest person in a nurse's attire.

"She's in labor and we need help immediately," Jake said.

"Sir, if your wife is in labor, you need to take her to the admission's office," the nurse explained. "After she's admitted, they'll take her up to her suite and her doctor will see her."

"I'll take her wherever she needs to go right now," Jake said, his deep voice a vicious growl. "Somebody can fill out the papers later!"

The ER nurse backed away from Jake, and Donna covered her mouth to suppress a giggle. The poor woman's face had gone deathly white and her brown eyes bulged.

Tallie, Peyton and Sheila flew into the ER behind Jake and Donna. Tallie grabbed Jake's arm and the nurse gasped as if she thought the big cowboy might strike the woman who had dared touch him.

"What's going on?" Tallie asked.

"Hank brought us to the wrong entrance," Sheila explained. "We need to go around to Admitting and fill out the paperwork so they can admit Donna."

The nurse sighed heavily, then smiled weakly at Sheila. "That's what I've been trying to tell this, er, gentleman. But he doesn't seem to want to cooperate."

"Cooperate be damned!" Jake roared the exclamation. "Donna's in labor!"

Cringing, the nurse backed farther away from Jake. Tallie shook her finger in her brother's face. "You're scaring the daylights out of—" Tallie examined the nurse's name badge "—Ms. Rivers. There are rules and regulations that she must—"

Donna moaned loudly as yet another pain ripped through

her. Jake's mouth tightened, his jaw clenched. His dark gaze zipped around the room in a search mode. He spotted someone he assumed was a doctor.

"Hey, Doc! I've got a woman in labor here—" he hoisted Donna a few inches higher to dramatize the situation "—and we need some help for her now, not later."

"Dr. Keifer, I tried to explain to this man—" Nurse Rivers said.

"First-time father?" the slender, bespectacled, young doctor asked as he approached Jake.

"Yes," three feminine voices replied—Sheila, Tallie and Donna.

Dr. Keifer grinned. Jake grunted. The doctor placed his hand on Jake's shoulder.

"I'm Stan Keifer, Mr...?"

"Bishop. Jake Bishop."

"Mr. Bishop, we're going to get a wheelchair for Mrs. Bishop—" The doctor motioned to the stunned nurse, who nodded and raced off to follow his instructions. "—And they'll take her on up to her suite while you go around to Admitting and fill out the paperwork."

"I'll have to fill out the paperwork," Donna said. "The insurance is in my name and—"

"Just give your husband your insurance card—" Dr. Keifer said.

"He's not my husband!" Donna turned to Jake, glaring at him. "You can put me down now! I'm perfectly capable of handling this myself."

Jake eased her onto her feet, but kept one arm around her.

The nurse returned with a wheelchair. Donna pulled away from Jake and sat immediately. "Let's go to admissions and get this show on the road."

Jake stood in the doorway, big, brooding and mouth agape.

Tallie grabbed the wheelchair handlebars and looked over her shoulder at her brother. "Let's go get Donna admitted before she has this baby in the hallway."

Jake felt like a fool. He was in unknown waters here, sailing an uncharted course. All he wanted was help for Donna—for the woman who was about to give birth to his child. The very thought of fatherhood overwhelmed him. The last thing on earth he had expected when he showed up for Hank's wedding was to find his weekend lover on the verge of childbirth.

Tallie tapped her foot. "Well? Are you coming with us or not?"

Without saying a word, Jake fell into line beside Peyton and Sheila and followed his sister as she wheeled Donna down the hall.

Fifteen minutes later the Bishop clan took up residence in Donna's suite in the hospital's separate maternity division. Jake stood in the corner, silent and sullen, refusing to answer any questions from his two younger brothers—and grateful that Tallie was too absorbed in Donna to harass him. Nobody could harass and needle better than his little sister. She'd been a hellcat even as a child. Maturity had mellowed her only slightly.

He watched with curiosity and concern as the nurses followed what was obviously standard procedure as they prepared Donna for childbirth. Before the family had been allowed into the suite, Donna had changed into a blue-and-white-striped cotton gown. She was now hooked up to a bag containing some kind of intravenous fluids—and to an electronic fetal monitor. That's what the nurse had called it when he'd asked.

''Dr. Farr!'' Donna held out her hand toward the middle-aged man who entered the room.

The doctor took Donna's hand, patted it in a reassuring manner and smiled broadly. ''Looks like we won't have to induce labor, after all. I'm glad this young lady decided to make her entrance into the world before she grows any larger. We wouldn't want you delivering an eleven pound baby, would we?''

''Eleven pounds?'' Susan asked.

''When they're full-term, Bishop babies tend to be large,'' Sheila said. ''Danny weighed almost ten pounds.'' She patted her belly. ''Lord only knows how big this one will be.''

''Yes, mine came in at over nine pounds,'' Tallie said, then glanced accusingly at Jake. ''Since this little girl's daddy is six-three and a pretty big guy, she'll be lucky to weigh less than ten pounds.''

While Jake's mind whirled with the news that his child would be a girl, the nurse shooed him and the Bishop clan out of the room while Dr. Farr examined Donna.

He'd never thought much about fatherhood, had never actually considered having children. But the few times the notion had crossed his mind, he'd imagined his child being a boy. After all, boys ran in the Bishop family. Caleb had a son. Tallie had two boys. Now Hank had a son.

Even though Jake had a difficult time picturing himself as a father, he supposed he'd figured that helping raise a little boy was something he could handle. But a little girl? God help him, a little girl was a different matter altogether. A baby girl would need gentleness and tenderness, probably more than a boy. And any daughter of Donna's would be a little lady. Jake would be the first to admit that he didn't know a damn thing about ladies, little or otherwise.

Dr. Farr stepped out into the hallway and glanced at the

seven adults waiting there. "Donna's labor is progressing quickly. I don't think we'll have a very long wait. Sheila, since you're Donna's coach, you should go on in and be with her now."

Sheila glanced over at Jake, who stared back at her in bewilderment. "I think the baby's father should be with her for the delivery."

"The baby's father?" Dr. Farr questioned. "I didn't realize that Donna had any contact with the father."

"She does now," Tallie said. "The father is here—" she pointed to her eldest brother "—and he's the type who likes to take charge of situations."

"I'm Dr. Farr, Mr...?"

"Jake Bishop."

"Hank and Caleb's brother?" the doctor asked.

"That's right."

"And you're the father of Donna's baby?"

"Looks that way."

"Do you want to be with Donna during the remainder of her labor and the delivery of your child?"

*Did he? Could he?* "Yeah, I want to be with her," he answered finally. No woman should go through childbirth without the baby's father, Jake thought. And no kid should grow up without a dad, the way he and his brothers and Tallie had.

Jake followed Dr. Farr back into Donna's room. The attendants turned and stared at him.

"This is Jake Bishop." The doctor introduced him. "He's the baby's father."

All the women smiled warmly and moved aside to allow him space next to the bed.

"What are you doing here?" Donna glared at him. "Where's Sheila?"

"Everybody thought I should be present for our daughter's birth," Jake replied.

"She's my daughter!"

"She's our daughter, sugar." Jake took Donna's hand in his and lifted it to his lips.

She narrowed her eyes and glowered at him. "You didn't even know she existed until a few hours ago! You have no right to make claims on my baby. You weren't supposed to be a part of her life. You're totally unsuitable to be Louisa Christine's father."

Jake kissed Donna's hand, then sat in a chair one of the attendants scooted over to him. "Louisa Christine sure is a mouthful for a little baby. Maybe we should call her Christy or Lou."

Donna jerked her hand away. "We will do no such thing. I'm naming her in honor of my grandmothers and I'm going to call her Louisa!"

"Sure thing. You call her whatever you want to call her."

"Don't you patronize me, J.B.! Dammit, I mean Jake."

"I don't mind you calling me J.B."

"That's not your name, is it? If you'd told me you were Jake Bishop the night we met, I wouldn't be in this situation now."

Jake leaned over, lifted his hand to Donna's face and caressed her moist cheek. "Are you sure about that, sugar? As I recall, nothing short of an act of God would have prevented what happened between us."

"Why you…you…you…" Donna spluttered furiously.

"Calm down," Jake said. "What will these fine folks here think if we keep fussing with each other?"

Donna glanced around the room at the attendants, who tried to pretend they weren't listening to every word of the not-so-private conversation. "Right this minute, I don't give a damn what anyone thinks."

Dr. Farr motioned to Jake. "Are you ready to be a father, Mr. Bishop?"

Was he ready to be a father? Hell, no! He'd been a renegade and a black sheep all his life. A hell-raiser, who had avoided responsibility and commitment for as long as he could remember. The last thing on earth he was ready for was fatherhood.

But prepared for the awesome task or not, he was about to have fatherhood thrust upon him. Without prior warning. With no preparation.

Jake stood, leaned over and kissed Donna's forehead. "I'm here for the duration, whether you want me or not."

Donna grabbed Jake's hand. He grasped tightly. They gazed into each other's eyes for a brief moment.

"I want you here," Donna admitted, doing a sudden about-face in attitude. "Don't leave me, Jake."

# Two

Following the last of Dr. Farr's instructions, Jake cut the umbilical cord. His heartbeat thundered in his ears as an exhilaration he'd never known rushed through his body.

"How about a good look at your daughter, Donna?" Dr. Farr indicated for the nurse to lay the newborn on Donna's abdomen. "She seems to be perfect in every way."

Jake stepped back, took a deep breath and gazed at the woman who had just given birth to his child. Despite the time in labor and with her makeup melted away, Donna was still beautiful. So beautiful that at that precise moment the sight of her and his infant daughter hit him like a sledgehammer to the gut.

Tears trickled down Donna's cheeks as she smiled. "Oh, my, isn't she beautiful?"

"Looks just like her daddy," one of the attendants said. "All that black hair and those big brown eyes. It's unusual for a baby to be born with such dark eyes."

A lump formed in Jake's throat and his heart skipped a beat. That tiny, wet, pink bundle that the nurse lifted from Donna's belly and held up for his inspection did look like him. This little girl was a Bishop, through and through.

The nurse cleaned Louisa Christine and dried her off, rubbing her briskly, then weighed and measured her. "Nine pounds, five ounces! And twenty-one inches long. She's a big girl."

The nurse quickly wrapped the baby in a warm, pink blanket and placed a cotton cap on her head. Jake watched in amazement as his daughter opened her little mouth and let out a piercing wail.

"Nothing wrong with her lungs, huh, Doc?" Jake said.

Dr. Farr nodded. The attendants laughed softly. Donna turned her head so that she could see her child while the doctor finished his work. Then she gazed up at Jake. "Will you go out and tell everyone that I'm all right and that Louisa is just perfect?"

"Sure thing."

"Will you come back after you've told them?"

Jake paused, walked over to the bed and wiped several damp strands of cinnamon hair from Donna's forehead. "I'm not going to leave you, sugar. I'll be around for as long as you need me."

Her smile was faint and the look in her eyes questioned his sincerity. He supposed she had no reason to trust him. After all, they barely knew each other. He was scarcely more than a stranger to the mother of his child.

"I'll let the folks know that there's a gorgeous new addition to the Bishop family." Jake headed for the door, stopped abruptly after he opened it, and glanced back over his shoulder. "I think maybe we should get married."

Before Donna had a chance to reply, he walked into the hall and closed the door behind him. Within seconds the

Bishop clan surrounded him, bombarding him with questions.

Warding them off with hand motions, Jake laughed. "Hey, cool it, y'all. Mother and daughter are fine. Donna came through like a trooper. And our daughter is one hundred percent Bishop. She weighs nine pounds and five ounces and she's twenty-one inches long. And she's got a mouth as loud as her aunt Tallie's."

Tallie punched his shoulder. "Smart aleck," she teased.

"When can we see them?" Sheila asked.

"As soon as they get through in there with Donna, I guess," Jake replied.

"Then you've got time to do some explaining," Tallie said. "Just how is it that our friend Donna wound up pregnant with your baby and nobody knew you were the father?"

Hank and Caleb laughed. Their wives gave them warning glances, which sobered them immediately.

Peyton Rand put his arm around his wife's shoulder and said, "Tallie, honey, I think it's fairly obvious that nine months ago Jake and Donna were together. And if I understand correctly what Susan has told us, Donna and Jake didn't bother to exchange last names or past histories at the time."

"Is that right?" Tallie tapped her foot on the shiny, wood-look tile floor.

"Yep," Jake said sheepishly. "Donna and I spent one weekend together and parted company. We didn't plan on ever seeing each other again. Believe me, I was startled when I saw her at Hank's wedding reception and shocked when I noticed she was very pregnant."

"Well, what do you plan to do about this situation?" Tallie crossed her arms over her ample chest and continued tapping her foot.

"What do you think I should do, little sister?"

"I think you should ask Donna to marry you—today!" Tallie pointed her finger up at Jake's face. "You may have been an irresponsible renegade all your life, but you're thirty-six years old. It's high time you settled down. You're a father now and that means you'll have to—"

"Let him have a breather," Caleb said. "Something tells me that Jake is going to do the right thing on his own, without your preaching him a sermon."

"Jake shouldn't marry Donna in order to do the right thing," Sheila said. "Marriage is about love and wanting to share the rest of your life with someone."

"We have to think of little Louisa Christine," Susan said. "The baby is the most important person in all this."

While his family made their feelings known—in no uncertain terms—Jake felt the heavy weight of reality fall on his shoulders. He had fathered a child. Nothing could change that fact. Just a few yards away, inside the Magnolia Suite, was a baby girl he had helped create one hot summer night in New Mexico. And there was a lady, whose reputation, when the whole truth came out, would, no doubt, be ruined in Marshall County.

The trouble was, he didn't know a damn thing about Donna. Hell, he still didn't know her last name. But if she was friends with his sister and sisters-in-law, then that meant she was probably a fine woman. His instincts told him that she was a thoroughbred, a true lady, which meant she probably wouldn't be interested in hitching up with a beat-up, uneducated cowboy whose greatest ambition in life was to own a quarter horse ranch.

But Tallie was right. He was thirty-six. He'd been an irresponsible drifter and hell-raiser most of his life. Maybe it was past time he settled down. Wasn't that one of the reasons he'd come home to Tennessee, why he'd made Old

Man Henry an offer on his ranch? He was tired of roaming. Tired of not having a home of his own. Tired of being alone.

Dr. Farr emerged from Donna's suite. "Y'all can go in and see the new mother and baby now." He placed his hand on Jake's shoulder. "I'm glad you were here for Donna during the delivery."

The Bishop clan descended upon Donna en masse, Hank, Caleb and Peyton standing back and observing as Susan, Sheila and Tallie circled the bed. Jake stood in the doorway, a hard ball of uncertainty lying heavily in the pit of his stomach.

Tallie eased over beside her newborn niece. "Oh, she is a beauty. Look at that mane of black hair and those big brown eyes. She's the spitting image of Jake!"

A numbing sensation spread quickly through Jake's body. He wanted to turn around and walk away, but his legs wouldn't cooperate. *You're not ready for this!* an inner voice warned. *What kind of father would you be? You don't know the first thing about babies, especially baby girls. Do that little girl and her mother a favor and get out of their lives.*

"Have you held her yet, Jake?" Tallie asked as she lifted the infant in her arms. "Come here and take your daughter."

Jake hesitated momentarily. All eyes were on him. He forced himself to move, to cross the room and accept the bundle that his sister offered him. His hands trembled. His arms stiffened. The tiny newborn felt weightless. What the hell was he doing? His gut tightened painfully.

Holding the infant as if she were made of glass, Jake gazed down at his daughter. *His daughter!* She wriggled. He tensed, then quickly offered her to Tallie.

"Here, do something with her before I drop her."

Tallie laughed, took the child from him and carried her over so that her other two aunts could coo over her adoringly. Jake watched while the women made a fuss over Louisa. Louisa Christine. He still thought the name was too much for a baby. He liked the idea of calling her Christy, but figured Donna wouldn't approve.

*What difference does it make anyway?* That inner voice asked. *You probably won't be a major part of her life. Unless you marry Donna.*

He glanced over at the bed just in time to see Donna take the baby in her arms. The picture was perfect. Madonna and child. Mother and daughter.

"You've got yourself a peach of a mother, kiddo," Jake said to himself. "A beautiful, classy lady. But I'm afraid your old man isn't much of a prize."

Susan lowered her infant son close to the newborn. "Lowell, I'd like to introduce you to your cousin, Louisa. You two are going to be really good friends."

"I think we should all leave and let the mama and papa have some time alone," Hank suggested. "We can come back tomorrow for another visit."

"I'll be going home tomorrow afternoon," Donna said. "Dr. Farr told me that there's no reason to keep me and Louisa more than twenty-four hours. That's pretty much hospital procedure these days."

"We'll come over to your house tomorrow night," Sheila said. "I'll bring supper and Susan and I can help you adjust to being home."

"Thanks. I'd appreciate that." Donna caressed little Louisa's rosy cheek. "I've hired a nanny, but she won't start work until next week."

Had he heard her correctly? Jake wondered. A nanny? If Donna could afford a nanny, that had to mean she had a job and money of her own. She wouldn't need him to help support their child.

But fathers are needed for more than financial support, he reminded himself. A kid needs a father around all the time, even a little girl.

Jake waited until his family had left before he approached Donna's bed. She seemed totally absorbed in her inspection of their child. He cleared his throat. She ignored him. He cleared his throat again—louder. She glanced up, a frown marring her pleasant features.

"I think maybe we should talk, don't you?" he said.

"What's there to talk about?"

"About you and me and—" he nodded toward the infant "—our child."

"She's my child, Jake. I've never thought of her any other way. I don't expect you to take any responsibility for her, if that's what you're worried about."

Heat rose up Jake's neck and spread across his face. Donna's comment pushed all the wrong buttons, bringing his temper to the boiling point.

"Dammit, woman! Did you ever stop to think I might want to take responsibility? That I might want to play a part in *my* daughter's life?"

That's what she'd been afraid of—that Jake Bishop might want to be a real father to her baby girl. Donna didn't want this big, roughneck cowboy to be a part of Louisa's life in any way. After their weekend in Plain City, she'd thought she would never see him again. Having a brief affair with the man was one thing, but having him become a permanent part of her life was another thing altogether!

"Yes, I did consider the possibility that you might want to be a part of Louisa's life, but I dismissed the notion," Donna said. "After all, you're hardly the type of man who'd want to be tied down to a woman and child. And there is the fact that you and I hardly know each other.''

"We spent two days and two nights together!" Jake's voice bellowed.

Louisa stirred in her mother's arms, then she whimpered. "Hush! You're scaring her." Donna glared menacingly at him. "During that two days and two nights, we didn't have one meaningful conversation.''

"Sugar, you weren't any more interested in conversation than I was. I gave you what you wanted. I gave it to you over and over again.''

Donna's amber eyes flashed golden fire. Her cheeks flared crimson. "You egotistical, macho jerk!"

Jake moved closer to her bedside, leaned over so that their faces were at the same level and smiled wickedly at her. "We should get married as soon as possible.''

"What!" Donna screamed the word.

Louisa whimpered, then cried. Donna cuddled the child close to her bosom and crooned comforting nonsensical words to her. She glared at Jake.

"Go away! I don't need you and I don't want you. And neither does Louisa.''

Jake cupped the back of his daughter's tiny head. It filled his huge palm. "Do you think it's that easy to get rid of me? I'm not going anywhere until we set up some ground rules concerning my daughter. And you're dead wrong if you think she doesn't need me or want me." He took the infant away from Donna and up into his arms. Trembling inside as if his body had been hit by an earthquake, Jake lifted the whimpering baby up against his chest, patted her back and said, "It's all right, Sugar Baby. Daddy's got you now.''

Donna looked up at the big man cradling Louisa against his chest and, for just a moment, couldn't breathe. The sight

of father and child overwhelmed her senses. There was
something so essentially right about the two of them together. Strength protecting helplessness. A powerful man
guarding what was his.

The awareness of Jake as her child's father surprised
Donna. She had tried not to think about J.B. during the
months she was carrying Louisa, though memories of that
weekend had often invaded her thoughts. And in the hours
since she'd learned her weekend lover was actually Jake
Bishop, she had refused to acknowledge the possibility that
he would play a significant part in her daughter's life.

But here he was now, as big, powerful and rugged as
he'd been the first night he'd held her in his arms at the
Blue Bonnet Grill—the night she'd lost her mind and succumbed to purely physical pleasure. She'd fought the memory of this man for nine months, but he had wreaked havoc
on her subconscious. How many nights had she awakened,
hot and aroused, after dreaming about him? Even now, only
hours after giving birth, she couldn't deny the strong attraction she felt for Jake. And the sight of his gentle hold
on her baby did crazy things to her heart.

"Jake, I think we should talk—really talk—about our
situation." Donna motioned for him to come to her.

Carrying Louisa in his arms, he walked over and sat on
the edge of the bed, then turned their daughter so that she
rested between them.

"I don't especially care for the name Louisa Christine,"
Jake said. "But as long as her last name is Bishop, I won't
object."

Donna clenched her teeth to keep from making a stinging
reply. Just what was wrong with her grandmothers's
names? "You want your name on her birth certificate?"

"Damn right I do! She's a Bishop and I want her name
to be Bishop on her birth certificate."

"All right," Donna agreed, rationalizing to herself that if she gave in to him on this matter, he might be more reasonable when it came to other things—things about which she wasn't willing to compromise.

"I'm going to stay the night with y'all tonight." Jake gazed down adoringly at Louisa. "I'll run over to Hank's in the morning to shower and shave and then I'll come back and take you and my sweet sugar baby home."

"That won't be necessary—" When she noticed the fury in Jake's dark eyes, she decided it was best to change tactics. "All right, you can stay the night and then take us home tomorrow afternoon. But when your family leaves, after supper, I expect you to leave, too."

"I'm going to be working for Old Man Henry out at his ranch for the next few months," Jake told her. "Once we get married, I can drive out there everyday, but when he sells the place to me, I'll want us to move out there and live on the ranch."

Live on a ranch? Around smelly horses? With a man she barely knew? She didn't think so.

"About our getting married—" she began.

"I'll give you some time to get used to the idea. I know you'll need to recuperate from giving birth and all, so let's set a date for six weeks from now." The corners of Jake's mouth curved into a devilish smile. "We wouldn't want to waste our wedding night."

Donna's cheeks flushed. Dammit, she was too old to be blushing, but the thought of a wedding night with Jake was almost more than she could bear. No matter how hard she tried, she couldn't forget what it had been like to be his lover for sixty of the most passionate, hedonistic and wildest hours of her life. She didn't know much about Jake Bishop, but she knew he was, without a doubt, an incredible lover.

"I'll agree to think about your marriage proposal over the next six weeks, but I'm afraid it's out of the question for you to live with Louisa and me."

Holding the back of her head securely, Jake lifted the baby up toward her mother. "Did you hear what Mommy said? She doesn't want me to live with y'all. What do you say to that, Sugar Baby?"

As if on cue, Louisa began to whimper. Jake grinned.

"Give her to me," Donna told him. "And wipe that silly grin off your face. The whimper wasn't a statement of her feelings toward your not living with us. She probably needs to be nursed."

"Nursed?"

"Yes, nursed. I'm breast-feeding Louisa."

Jake felt as if he'd been poleaxed between the eyes. The thought of his child at Donna's breast created an array of emotions inside him. Surprise. Tenderness. Arousal. Curiosity.

He handed the baby over to her mother. "Here you go, Sugar Baby. Mama's serving dinner."

Donna groaned. What a typically crude male thing to say! *Mama's serving dinner,* indeed! "Please stop calling Louisa 'Sugar Baby.' Nicknames often stick. She'd be terribly embarrassed if children at school called her such a silly, juvenile name."

"I don't care for the name Louisa and you've already vetoed Lou and Christy." Jake rose from the side of the bed. "She's my sweet sugar baby and that's what I'm going to call her."

Donna huffed. "Oh, all right. But for now, just go away." She shooed him with one hand. "Go eat dinner or buy some cigars or something."

"You're right. I should buy some cigars before Hank and Caleb come back to the hospital." Jake headed toward the door, paused, turned and grinned at Donna. "Maybe I'll buy the pink bubble gum kind, since the Bishop brothers don't smoke."

Donna breathed a sigh of relief when Jake finally left her room. Whenever she was around him, she felt as if she were caught in the swirl of a cyclone that swept her far from the safety of home. There was something about him— something primeval—that overwhelmed her whenever they were together.

She couldn't let him take charge of her life, push her into a marriage she didn't want and destroy the life she had planned for herself and Louisa. Once she'd settled in at home and had gained back her strength, she would confront Jake and explain to him how disastrous it would be for them to marry. There was no way on earth a marriage between them could work. From what she knew of Hank and Caleb Bishop's big brother, she realized that he wasn't the type of man she wanted to spend the rest of her life with, nor was he the kind of father Louisa would need. Better no father than a wild hellion womanizer, who'd never be able to settle down and be a faithful husband and devoted parent.

Jake pulled out his credit card, handed it to the salesclerk at the florist shop in the Marshallton Mall and waited for her to ring up his order. He knew that if he were going to persuade Donna to marry him, he'd have to woo her first. He hadn't ever really thought about marriage. Not seriously. He'd figured that he was meant to die an old bachelor. But having a child changed all that. His own father had been a worthless bum and his grandfather had been a stern, cold care-giver. He wanted better for his daughter. Sugar Baby deserved a devoted, full-time father. A man who'd be around when she needed him. And the only way he could give his baby girl what she needed most from him was by marrying her mother.

He didn't kid himself about the chances for a happy marriage. Donna wasn't in love with him and he wasn't in love with her. But the sex they'd shared had been damn good, some of the best he'd ever had. And marriages had succeeded on far less. He was past the age to expect both passion and love in a relationship. He'd be more than happy to settle for passion—and possession of his child and the woman who'd given birth to her.

"We'll deliver those to your wife's suite this evening, Mr. Bishop," the blond salesclerk said. "She's going to love two dozen pink roses."

"I hope she does."

"She will." The young woman smiled flirtatiously at Jake. "Congratulations on becoming a father. I take it, from your ordering pink roses, that it was a girl."

Jake grinned broadly. "Yep. Nine pounds, five ounces. And she looks just like me."

"Lucky little girl. She must be beautiful."

"Ah, shucks, ma'am, you'll make me blush," Jake said. "By the way, do you happen to know where the nearest toy store is?"

"Toyland is on the second level here at the mall. Just take the escalator and it's the third store on the outside right."

"Thanks." Jake signed the sales slip, pocketed his credit card and tipped his Stetson to the smiling clerk.

Within half an hour, Jake had chosen the items he wanted, paid for them and headed back to the hospital. When he arrived outside Donna's suite, a giant pink teddy bear under one arm and two big baby dolls under the other, he met his brothers.

"Well, well, what have we here?" Caleb asked. "Looks like the proud new papa has been on a shopping spree."

"Where's your women folk?" Jake asked. "And Tallie and Peyt?"

"Peyton had an emergency at the capitol, so he had to rush back to Nashville," Hank said. "Tallie went with him. She said to tell you and Donna that she'd be back for the christening or the wedding, whichever comes first."

"Sheila and Susan are in there with Donna," Caleb said. "They're admiring the roses you sent. I think they're trying to persuade the mother of your child that you aren't such a bad guy."

A plump, middle-aged nurse's aide rolled a cart past the Bishop brothers, paused outside the door to the Magnolia Suite and sized up the three men. "Which one of you is the daddy?"

"Me," Jake replied.

"Well, come on in and join your wife for a steak dinner, compliments of the Marshallton Women's Center." She opened the door and rolled the cart inside, all the while whistling to herself.

"A steak dinner, huh?" Jake followed the aide into the suite.

He stopped dead in his tracks when he saw Donna sitting propped up against several pillows. She'd brushed her hair and pinned it to the top of her head. Wispy strands curled about her face, to which she had applied a light coating of makeup. Lipstick and blush in some bright shade of pink colored her lips and cheeks. And she wore a hot pink satin bed jacket.

She was the prettiest thing he'd ever seen. An auburn-haired angel with a body that would tempt the devil. She was still a little swollen and her face was still round from

the pregnancy, but the abundance of her curves did nothing
to lessen her attractiveness.

He might not know much about the mother of his child,
but he knew one thing—just looking at her turned him inside out. And by the way she glanced past her friends and
focused on him, he had a feeling that he affected her the
same. The smile on her face vanished. Her eyes widened.
Her lips parted slightly. Damn! He wanted to kiss her.

The sight of Jake Bishop standing tall and proud in the
doorway set off a firestorm along Donna's nerve endings.
He was so big and rugged and dangerously handsome that
she couldn't take her eyes off him.

"Hello, Jake." She knew her voice sounded soft and
raspy and wished she could take back the greeting. Would
he read something into the way she'd spoken to him, something she'd been unable to hide?

"There you are," Sheila said. "We were wondering
when you'd get back here."

"What have you got under your arms?" Susan asked.

"What? Oh, these." Jake lifted the teddy bear up to
show them, then placed it in a nearby chair. He took a doll
in each hand, walked over to the portable plastic crib where
little Louisa lay and held up the dolls for her inspection.

"Daddy brought his girl a teddy bear and a couple of
baby dolls. What do you think of these dolls, Sugar Baby?"

"She's too young to talk," Sheila kidded him.

"Here, Mr. Bishop, let me put those on the table beside
Louisa's crib." The nurse's aide reached for the dolls Jake
held. "Then you and Ms. Fields can enjoy your dinner
together."

"Isn't that a wonderful idea," Susan sighed. "Serving
the parents a steak dinner in the mother's suite the night
their baby's born. Hank and I missed that treat."

"Absolutely wonderful idea." Sheila tugged on Susan's

arm. "Let's join our husbands and see if they'll take us out to eat since we've got a baby-sitter for tonight."

"Y'all don't have to rush off," Donna said.

"We'll see you tomorrow evening at your house," Sheila reminded her. "I'm bringing dinner, remember."

Donna watched helplessly as her best friends departed and the nurse's aide left her alone with the one man on earth she didn't want anywhere near her. Jake made her act irresponsibly. Around him, she didn't think rationally. Nine months ago, she'd acted totally out of character when Jake had taken her into his arms. And she'd wound up pregnant, unmarried and forced to concoct a totally unbelievable story about a whirlwind marriage and quickie divorce. Now he was back in her life, laying claim to her and to Louisa. The man had asked her to marry him. What was she going to do? She had to get him out of her life before, in a weak moment, she accepted his proposal.

Jake lifted the plastic covers from the plates. "This sure looks good, sugar. Why don't I put both dinners on your little portable table there and I'll drag up a chair."

*Go away,* she wanted to scream. *Leave me alone. Stop being so nice and caring and concerned. I don't want to like you. I don't want to find you irresistible. I can't love you, Jake Bishop. Not now or ever. I'm never going to love a man again. I've loved and lost once and it nearly killed me. I won't risk knowing that kind of pain ever again.*

Afraid to speak for fear she might voice her concerns, she watched him silently as he set the plates down on the table and rolled it up to the bed. When she finally found her voice again, she said, "Thank you for the roses. You shouldn't have. I know they must have been terribly expensive."

"Nothing's too good for you, Donna." Jake shrugged. "Besides, it's not like I couldn't afford them. I'm not a rich man by any means, but I'm not exactly penniless, either."

"No, of course, you're not. I didn't mean to imply that I thought—"

"You like them, right? That's all that matters."

"Jake?"

"What?"

"It won't work, you know—a marriage between the two of us. We'd mix like oil and water. I realize we don't know anything about each other, but I have a feeling we have nothing in common."

"We've got a couple of things in common," he said as he pulled a chair up beside her bed.

"What do we have in common?"

"First of all, we've got a daughter. Your child and mine."

"Well, yes, there is that, but—"

"And we've got this!" Jake leaned over, circled her neck with his big hand and pulled her toward him. Before she had a chance to protest, he kissed her.

By the time he finished, Donna was breathless. She stared at him with dazed eyes. "Yes, there is that, too." Then she reached out, pulled him back down to her and kissed him as soundly and as thoroughly as he had her.

# Three

Jake had insisted on driving mother and child home from the hospital in his Jeep. As he pulled up alongside Donna's sleek little Corvette in the driveway of an address in one of Marshallton's more prestigious neighborhoods, he realized the ten-year-old truck he had bought from Hank didn't begin to compare. What bothered him more than the difference in their vehicles, however, was Donna's house. A white, two-story Colonial in the historical district of Marshallton. Obviously, the woman had money. Which meant she didn't need financial support from him. He'd seen the farmhouse at the Henry Ranch and it didn't hold a candle to Donna's place on Mulberry Lane. Even if they remodeled the farm house from top to bottom, would Donna ever be satisfied living there?

What could he offer a woman who apparently had everything? he wondered. Probably nothing she wanted or didn't already have.

The balloon bouquet Susan had tied to the lamppost
bounced in the evening breeze. Sheila opened the front
door, which was decorated with a huge pink balloon, and
ushered them inside. The smell of barbecue greeted their
senses as they entered the house. Jake's brothers stood in
the foyer, below the pink-and-white banner that read Louisa
Christine Bishop. Their Little Miss Bishop's homecoming
had turned into a major celebration. Caleb and Hank took
turns videotaping the whole affair and the family replayed
the tape twice before they left.

Jake gazed down at his daughter, asleep in her basinet.
*I can't give your mama anything she wants or needs. What
about you? What can I give you, Sugar Baby? What does
a little girl need most?*

Donna waved goodbye to the Bishops, closed the front
door and returned to the den where Jake stood over
Louisa's basinet, watching his sleeping daugther. Donna
wished that he wasn't so fascinated with their baby. He
didn't seem like the type of man who'd go all mushy inside
over an infant, especially a female infant. But what did she
know about Jake? Nothing really. Maybe he'd always
wanted a child or maybe he had a soft spot in his heart for
little girls.

"I'm really tired, Jake. I think I should take Louisa to
my room and go to bed myself." She paused several feet
away from him, waiting for him to look up and acknowledge her presence.

He glanced at her, smiled and nodded his head. "I'll
wheel the basinet to your room, if you'll just show me the
way."

Donna hesitated. Oh, what the heck! "All right. But I'll
carry Louisa. You'll have to lift the basinet to bring it upstairs. That's where my bedroom is."

"Sure thing. No problem." He removed the sleeping infant from the basinet, handed her to Donna and then picked up the eyelet-lace-adorned basinet.

Donna ascended the stairs slowly, her body still in a state of recovery from the recent delivery. Jake followed her, adjusting his pace to hers. The minute he entered Donna's private domain, he stopped, let out a long, low whistle and shook his head. The room possessed the same elegance and style as the woman, and was as far removed from his life-style as Donna was from the women he'd known over the years.

Donna eased her sore, weary body down onto her bed and waited for Jake to bring the basinet closer. But he didn't move. He just stopped in the doorway, his gaze scanning the area from the corona over the Louis XVI bed to the French doors that led out onto a small balcony over-looking the backyard garden.

From the expression on Jake's face, she surmised that he wasn't accustomed to ladies' bedrooms being filled with expensive antiques. No doubt, most of Jake's "experiences" with women had taken place in cheap motel rooms.

*Like the motel room you shared with him for a weekend!* a little voice mocked.

"Please, place the basinet right here—" she indicated the spot by pointing to it "—by my bed. With her this close, I won't have to get up during the night to feed her and change her diaper."

Jake put the basinet beside the bed, then turned to Donna. "Well, I don't guess I can feed her, but I suppose I can change her diaper...if you'll show me how."

Donna gazed at him quizzically. "I don't think that will be necessary."

"Sure it is. I've never changed a diaper before in my life. And Hank said you'll need all the rest you can get for the next couple of days and nights, so I should take over diaper duty for the time being.''

''Hank said…'' Donna let her sentence trail off as she realized that Jake had every intention of spending the night. So, that's why Sheila hadn't stayed, as they had originally planned—back in the good old days, before Jake had come to town!

How was she going to tell him that he couldn't spend the night? She'd have to send him away and then call Sheila. She would need help for the next few days, until the nanny she'd hired started work. Maybe she could call Mrs. Winthrop to see if she could start a few days early.

''Jake, there's really no need for you to stay tonight,'' Donna said, deliberately avoiding eye contact with him.

''You're going to need somebody around for a day or two, until you and Sugar Baby settle in and adjust. Who better than our girl's daddy to help take care of her?''

''Jake, I… Well, this is Marshallton, Tennessee, you know. If you stay here, people are bound to talk and—''

Jake laughed. ''Sugar, don't you think the whole county is already buzzing with the news that old renegade Jake Bishop is your baby's daddy? You can't be naive enough to think you can keep something like that a secret.''

Donna sighed loudly. He was right, of course. Oh, God! What would her society friends and college associates think when they found out that Louisa's father was an uncouth, macho cowboy? No one except Joanie Richardson, who had quit her job and moved to California during the Christmas holidays, had an inkling about the complete true story behind Louisa's conception.

''All right, let's compromise.'' Donna eased herself to the edge of the bed, leaned over and nestled a still sleeping Louisa into the basinet. Forcing her tired legs to stand, she faced Jake. ''You can stay here tonight—in the bedroom across the hall. But I want you gone after breakfast in the morning. I'm going to call to see if Mrs. Winthrop can start work tomorrow instead of next week.''

Jake frowned, shifted nervously from one booted foot to the other and then cleared his throat. ''You aren't going to marry me, are you?''

Surprised by his statement, Donna hesitated before she replied. ''No, Jake, I'm not going to marry you.''

''I don't exactly fit in to all of this, do I?'' His gaze quickly surveyed the room. ''Hank told me that you're a college professor and that your folks are old money in these parts. I knew, that very first night, that you were a lady. I just didn't know you were a blue-blooded Southern belle.''

''It's not that I think I'm too good to marry you, it's just—''

''That I'm not good enough to marry you.''

''No, Jake, really… We are strangers, with nothing in common…except Louisa and…and—''

''A strong physical attraction?''

''Yes, something like that.'' Sitting on the edge of the bed again, Donna glanced away, so that Jake couldn't see just how strongly she still felt that physical attraction.

Jake thought she looked fragile and weary resting there on her blue-striped bedspread. Her eyelids drooped. She placed her hand over her mouth to cover a yawn.

''I'm staying tonight. And I'll help you, if you'll let me.'' Jake balled his hands into fists to keep from reaching out and caressing Donna's cheek. ''Even an old hard-ass like me should be able to change a diaper or rock a crying baby.''

''You're going to want to be a part of Louisa's life, aren't you?'' Having a father participate in her daughter's upbringing had not been part of Donna's plans. The only man with whom she'd ever wanted to share the responsibilities of parenthood had been Edward. Her husband. A man she had admired, respected and loved.

"The thought of my being involved in our little girl's raising bothers you, doesn't it?" Jake sat beside Donna on the bed. She immediately scooted away from him. He grunted. "You can't change the fact that I'm her father, you know. But maybe if I wasn't around, you could pretend her daddy was some guy like your dead husband. Somebody with education and breeding. Somebody you aren't ashamed of!"

Donna gasped. Her face paled. "I suppose Sheila or Susan told you about Edward." Talking to Jake about Edward seemed wrong somehow, as if by just mentioning Edward's name to this man was somehow a betrayal of all she and her husband had once shared.

"Yeah. Susan told me about him."

"I'm sorry," Donna said. "I realize that I haven't been very considerate of your feelings. But you have to understand that having you show up the way you did—so…so unexpectedly—upset all my plans. If you want to be a part of Louisa's life, then I'm sure we can come to some sort of understanding."

Jake crossed his arms, rested them on his chest and nodded several times. "I guess we're talking about visitation rights and stuff like that?"

"Yes, I suppose." She sighed. "Couldn't we wait and discuss this in the morning? I really am awfully tired." Without thinking, she reached over and laid her hand on his arm. The moment she touched him, his muscles tightened. Warmth spread from his body into her hand and then radiated through her whole body.

He turned abruptly, accidently knocking her hand aside. He stood, then reached down and helped her to her feet.

Taking her by the shoulders, he pivoted her slowly and pointed her in the direction of the bathroom.

"Go change into your gown. I'll keep an eye on Sugar Baby."

Donna groaned inwardly. Apparently Jake was determined to use that ridiculous nickname and there really wasn't anything she could do about it. At least, not tonight.

"All right. Thanks."

She hurried into the bathroom, stripped out of her slacks and loose blouse, which Susan had brought to the hospital this morning. Her soft, cotton gown hung on the peg behind the door. After removing it from the peg, she stepped into it and secured the buttons. While she was pregnant, she had purchased several large gowns that buttoned up the front, knowing she could continue using them once her baby arrived.

After slipping into her white satin house slippers and putting on her quilted white robe over the yellow-flowered gown, she emerged from the bathroom. The first thing she noticed was that all the lights were off, except one bedside lamp. The second thing she noticed was that her bed had been turned down. And the third thing she noticed was that Jake had taken off his boots and shirt and was sitting in the overstuffed Victorian chair in the corner of the room. Louisa, sans blanket, lay atop his hairy chest.

Donna swallowed, then took a deep, calming breath. The man had made himself at home! He was partially undressed and had removed Louisa from her basinet. How dare he! Just who did he think he was?

*Louisa's father,* a pesky inner voice reminded her. *Louisa's father and your lover.*

Donna's heart sank. How had this happened? How had all her well-laid plans gone haywire? Jake Bishop had shown up, out of nowhere, and turned out to be the mysterious J.B. That's what had gone wrong.

"She was whimpering a little, so I thought it best for me to reassure her that her daddy's here and she's safe."

Jake grinned and Donna's tummy flip-flopped. Stop it! she told herself. Do not let his sexy body and flirtatious smile lure you into accepting him into your life. You do not want this man! You do not need this man!

*Liar,* that damn pesky little voice said.

"I should change her diaper and then nurse her," Donna told him. "And I'd like a little privacy."

"Look, sugar, there's no need to be shy around me," Jake said, sitting up straight. He shifted Louisa so that she rested higher on his chest. "I've seen it all, remember?"

Donna noticed that Jake's jeans were unbuttoned. A shiver raced up her spine. Her femininity tightened and released as it recalled the intense pleasure this man's big, hard body had given her.

"Yes, I remember. But that doesn't mean you can—"

"I'm sleeping in here with you," he said. "I can't be of much help with Sugar Baby if I'm across the hall. I sleep like the dead, so I wouldn't hear you if you called me. But if you touch me, I'll wake instantly."

She stomped her foot. "Dammit, will you stop calling her 'Sugar Baby.' Her name is Louisa. Do you hear me? L-o-u-i-s-a!"

Jake took a thorough inventory of Donna as she glared at him. She had loosened her mane of mahogany-red hair. It fell down her back and across her shoulders like strands of fire. Her large, milk-filled breasts rose and fell with each labored breath. He wanted to watch her feed their child. He wanted to caress her and taste her sweetness for himself.

"Come on and show me how to change *Louisa*'s diaper,'' he said, emphasizing the baby's name. ''Then we can go to bed and you can nurse her and get her to sleep.''

''You are not sleeping in the bed with me!''

''Yes, I am.''

''No, you are not!''

''Who's going to stop me?''

''I'll call…'' Who would she call? Not Hank or Caleb. And certainly none of her colleagues. ''I'll call the police!''

''No, you won't. Just think of the scandal,'' Jake said.

''If you touch me, I'll…I'll kill you.''

Jake stood, walked across the room and laid Louisa down on the bed. ''Show me how to change her diaper.''

''Did you hear me?'' Donna planted her hands on her hips.

''I know we can't have sex until you recover from having my baby. I'm not some brute who's going to force himself on you.'' Jake fumbled with the pack of diapers lying on the nightstand, ripped open the wrong end and finally retrieved a diaper. ''I'm going to sleep beside you tonight, but I won't touch you. When Louisa needs you, I'll hand her over to you. Otherwise, you rest and let me take care of my daughter.''

Donna removed her robe, tossed it on the foot of the bed and walked over to stand beside Jake. ''Unsnap her sleeper, then open the Velcro tabs on her diaper and take it off.'' Donna demonstrated by doing, then she pointed to a square box on the nightstand beside the package of diapers. ''There are wipes in there, just pull one out, clean her little bottom, then dispose of both diaper and wipe in the Diaper Genie—'' She removed a wipe, then pointed to a pink-and-white contraption in the corner. ''After that, slip a new diaper under her, adjust the tabs, fold them like this—'' she pulled his big hand down and allowed him to finish the process ''—and it's that simple.''

"I suppose a dirty diaper is more complicated, huh?" Jake teased.

Donna didn't smile. She was furious with him and was certain he knew it. She snapped Louisa's sleeper closed, lifted the child into her arms, kicked off her house slippers and eased herself into bed, sliding her legs under the light covers.

"Will you at least have the decency to turn your back while I nurse Louisa?" Donna began unbuttoning her gown.

"I want to watch while you nurse her." Jake's voice possessed a deep, smoky sensuality.

Donna shivered. "Please, Jake, I'd rather..."

Jake sat on the edge of the mattress, reached over and finished unbuttoning her gown, then he spread it apart and looked at the nursing bra Donna wore. He studied it momentarily before he glanced up into her face. Her lips were slightly parted. Her eyes were wide and focused on his hands. Her cheeks flushed.

He unsnapped the hook that held the flap in place, then lowered the flap to reveal Donna's swollen breast.

Sucking in her breath, Donna gazed directly into Jake's eyes. A dozen different warring emotions exploded inside her. A part of her wanted to scream at him, to tell him he had no right to be here, no right to look at her, to touch her—to be a part of these special moments with Louisa. But another part of her, a part she didn't understand, wanted to share this moment with him, wanted him to look at her and touch her and be the loving husband and father every new mother wanted.

But he's not my husband! she thought to herself.

*Ah, but he could be,* that pesky little inner voice argued.

Trying to avoid Jake's perusal, Donna lifted Louisa to her breast, tickled the baby's cheek and helped her newborn find the nipple. Louisa latched on greedily and sucked for a couple of minutes, then paused as if tired. Donna readjusted her daughter in her arms and Louisa began nursing again.

Jake didn't think he'd ever seen a more beautiful sight in his life. A man would have to have a heart of stone not to be touched by the sight of his child at her mother's breast.

He was hard as a rock and about as aroused as a man could get, but despite his body's hunger, he was satisfied for the time being. Not only had Donna not kicked him out of her house, she had allowed him to stay in her bedroom. And he was going to sleep in the bed beside her tonight. She probably had no idea how much she'd given him by simply accepting his demands. He'd known—in his gut— that she didn't want him to leave. Despite what she'd said, he'd seen the need in her eyes. The need for her child's father to stay with her. If she had persisted in her attempts to send him away, of course he would have gone. But she hadn't been persistent and he was damned grateful.

Jake stood, removed his socks and jeans, nudged Donna over and got into bed on the left side where he'd placed Louisa's basinet. Donna glanced at him. He reclined his big body, squirmed to find a comfortable position, and then rested his head on the feather pillow.

"When she's finished, just hand her over to me and I'll put her down," Jake said. "If she wakes up, I'll take care of her, unless she wants to be fed again."

"Would you mind turning off the lamp?" Donna asked. "I have a night-light that should give off enough light."

"Sure thing." Jake turned off the lamp, flipped over onto his side and continued watching mother and child. "Thanks for letting me stay."

Donna cleared her throat. "I suppose, on some level, I

wanted you to stay,'' she admitted. ''But that doesn't mean I'm going to marry you or that we have a future together.''

''Other than as Louisa's parents.''

''Right…other than as Louisa's parents.''

Ten minutes later Donna handed her daughter to Jake, who kissed Louisa's cheek and laid her in the basinet.

''Sleep tight, Sugar Baby,'' he said, then lay down, turned his back to Donna and pulled the covers up over his shoulders.

Donna awoke to the sound of Louisa's cries and the shower running. Lifting her head from the pillow, she stared at the open bathroom door. Jake was in there, in the shower—naked! When he finished, he would open the shower door and step out—naked. He would stand there in all his masculine glory.

Louisa's continued bellowing—and it was bellowing, not a soft ladylike mewing that some babies make—brought Donna's attention back to her child. She scooted across the bed, lifted Louisa into her arms and spread kisses over the infant's face. Immediately, Louisa stopped yelling and began rooting at Donna's breast.

''Are you ready for breakfast, my sweet?'' Preparing her clothing quickly, Donna put the child to her breast. Louisa clasped the nipple. ''Now, Miss Louisa, you and I need to have a talk about this very loud, very boisterous crying you've been doing. It's highly inappropriate for a young lady to make so much noise.''

Louisa continued nursing, completely oblivious to her mother's instructions. Donna laughed, then glanced toward the shower. ''Of course, I suppose with that man—'' she inclined her head toward the bathroom ''—as your father, you've inherited some rather aggressive genes. Your aunt Tallie has never been quiet and ladylike in her life. Lord knows, if you take after your father's side of the family, you'll be emptying birdshot into some guy's backside by the time you're sixteen.''

''What's this about Sugar Baby shooting some guy with birdshot?'' Jake asked as he emerged from the bathroom, a towel draped around his hips.

Donna gasped. Louisa released her nipple. Jake stood in the doorway and smiled.

''Aren't y'all a pretty sight this morning,'' he said.

''I was just rambling to Louisa, telling her something about her aunt Tallie.'' Donna placed her nipple back in Louisa's mouth and the child began nursing again.

''If Sug—er, Louisa—turns out to be anything like Tallie, then we're going to have our hands full, aren't we?''

*We?* He'd said *we.* Donna realized that she couldn't put off talking to Jake any longer. She had to make him understand that, although he was Louisa's biological father, she and he were not a ''we.'' And she wasn't quite sure what kind of role he would play in Louisa's life.

She glanced at him as he picked up his clothes from the floor. ''Jake?''

''Yeah?'' He looked at the clothes he held in his hand. ''Oh, don't worry. I'll get dressed in the bathroom.''

''Thanks, but…oh, all right. After you're dressed, I'd like to talk to you.''

''Sure thing.''

By the time Jake returned, fully clothed, his hair dried and combed, Donna had changed Louisa's diaper and placed her back in the basinet. She sat at the foot of the bed, her hands folded neatly in her lap. Be succinct, she told herself. Get straight to the point.

Jake emerged with a smile on his face. Donna decided she preferred him without the smile. Sullen and frowning, she could resist him. But wearing that broad, heart-stopping smile made him much too appealing.

"Is she asleep?" he asked, walking lightly toward the basinet.

"No, she's just…"

Jake leaned over the basinet and ran a caressing forefinger around Louisa's face. "She's a beaut, isn't she? She may have my coloring, but I think she looks like you."

"Jake, we really must talk."

Jake sat beside her, slipped his arm around her waist and nuzzled her neck. "So, talk. But I'd rather be kissing you than talking to you."

She slapped his hands and shoved at his chest. "We have to talk. Now!"

"I'm not going to like this, am I?"

"Oh, Jake, why do you have to be the kind of man who wants to be a part of Louisa's life? I never dreamed a guy like you would be interested in fatherhood."

"Just what is 'a guy like me'?" Jake's smile faded quickly.

"Well, someone who's been a loner all his life. A ladies' man. A tough cowboy who left home before he'd even graduated from high school. A man who—"

Jake shot up off the bed. "A man who isn't good enough for you. Isn't that what you're trying to say?"

"Please, don't twist my words."

"Yeah, well, tell me this Ms. College Professor—if I had a college degree and a hefty bank account and had some etiquette book memorized, wouldn't you be interested in marrying me? In my being a full-time father to our child?"

"The truth is, that, no matter what, I wouldn't marry you. I was married once and I lost my husband five years ago. I'll never love another man. Edward's death destroyed my ability to love."

"You're still in love with your dead husband?"

"Yes." It was a lie, but perhaps if Jake believed she still loved Edward, he wouldn't pursue the idea of marriage. Love and marriage frightened her now. She would never allow herself to love someone so much that losing him could nearly destroy her. She couldn't bear that kind of agony again. Once had been more than enough for a life-time.

Jake wanted to grab her and shake her until her teeth rattled. Loving a dead man was such a waste. Donna was beautiful, vibrant and sensual. She was the kind of woman who needed a man—a man's adoration, his protection and his love. She was a woman who should be loved often and well. He wanted to be that man.

He'd like to tell her that he might have left Crooked Oak nearly eighteen years ago without obtaining his high school diploma, but that he was a world traveler and widely read. She'd be shocked if she realized just how much money he had in the bank. Enough to pay cash for Old Man Henry's quarter horse ranch. Enough to send Sugar Baby to college, too. But let Donna assume he was a stupid, penniless cow-poke who was going to beg a loan from the bank to buy the ranch. Still, it hurt him to think she might look at him like everyone else in Marshall County had.

"Jake, I think maybe we should wait a few days, until I've had a chance to recuperate and then we can decide exactly what part you should play in Louisa's life."

"You're probably right. With your hormones all wild and crazy, you might say or do something you'll regret later."

She nodded agreement. "Let's give ourselves a week, all right?"

"A week's fine with me."

"You can call as often as you'd like and check on Louisa."

"I take this to mean you don't want me to stay here with you?" Narrowing his gaze, Jake focused his attention directly on Donna's face. "All right, I'll move out to the ranch. I'm going to be working for Old Man Henry until the sale goes through. But a daily phone call won't cut it. I'll drop by every day to see my daughter."

"Is that necessary?"

"Yeah, it's more than necessary. It's essential. For me and for Sugar Baby."

Donna huffed and took a deep breath that sucked in her cheeks. "You aren't going to make this easy for either of us, are you?"

"I've been taking the easy way out all my life, but not now, not about this. I'm going to be a real father to my daughter and whether you like it or not, I'm going to be a major part of her life and yours."

"Even if I don't want you in our lives?"

"Sugar, you want me in your life—you just don't know it yet."

With that said, Jake walked over, took a last look at his daughter and left the bedroom. Donna jumped up and rushed out into the hallway. She watched as Jake took the steps two at a time. She wanted to call out to him, to tell him that hell would freeze over before she'd ever want him in her life on a permanent basis, but the words died on her lips.

It wasn't that she didn't want Jake. She did. Her body, even now, yearned for his. It wasn't that she couldn't accept him as Louisa's father, no matter what his background. The honest truth was that she was scared senseless. Afraid that if Jake Bishop stayed in her life, she'd wind up falling in love with him.

# Four

Although Donna knew Louisa was in good hands with Mrs. Winthrop, she felt guilty for having left her two-week-old daughter, even for the few hours it would take to tie up loose ends at the office. The spring quarter had ended and although she wasn't teaching any classes this summer, she had no intention of giving up her position at the college. When Edward died, teaching had been her lifeline, the day-to-day contact with others that had kept her sane. She loved teaching. For her, being an educator was a true calling, not just a job, as it was for many others.

Even with Jake Bishop a daily visitor, Donna had been able to put her life back on an even keel since Louisa's birth. She prided herself on always being in control. Friends told her she was a *control freak*. The first week had been less than perfect, too much company, not enough sleep. But the second week had passed more smoothly. Despite Louisa being a little angel, Donna didn't think she could get along without Mrs. Winthrop. The warm, friendly, motherly woman knew all there was to know about babies. She was a completely different sort of woman from the nannies her parents had hired to care for her when she was a child. Donna's parents had been too involved in their careers and social life to personally oversee the upbringing of their only child—an unexpected, unwanted surprise, who came to them in their forties.

The one thing Donna intended to do every day of Louisa's life was to tell her daughter that she was loved and wanted. The only true maternal influences in Donna's life had been her grandmothers. The happiest moments of her childhood had been visiting Gram—Louisa McGuire— a woman who baked cookies, told fabulous stories and let her grandchild dress up in her hats and shoes. Her other grandmother—Christine Hughes—had also taken a keen interest in Donna. Far more than either parent. She had introduced Donna to the opera and the ballet, concerts and art museums, and had chaperoned her first trip to Europe.

A loud tap on the outer door of her office erased those sweet memories from Donna's mind. "Yes?"

The door opened and Neil Webster peered into the office. "Hello, there. I heard you'd come in today. How are things going?"

"Hello, Neil." Donna groaned silently. Neil was the financial aide director for the community college. A nice man, he tended to be a nosy busybody. He knew everyone's business and loved spreading gossip.

He slipped into the office and closed the door behind him. "The place is abuzz about your former *husband* showing up unexpectedly. I understand he's some sort of cowboy and he's Governor Rand's brother-in-law."

"That's right." Fully prepared to perpetuate the lie that she and Jake had been married briefly last summer, Donna plastered a phony smile onto her face. "Jake Bishop is back in Crooked Oak and is looking into buying a quarter horse ranch there."

"Everyone's curious as to whether you and Mr. Bishop will remarry." Neil leaned over Donna's desk, lowered his voice and whispered, "You know, of course, that some people are saying y'all were never married. President Harper's wife was terribly upset when she heard the rumor. I assured her that it wasn't true."

"Thank you, Neil." Donna cast her gaze heavenward and prayed for someone to rescue her from this well-meaning friend.

Resting a hip on the desk as he leaned closer, Neil glanced from side to side, as if checking for hidden spies. "Between the two of us, my dear, if there's any truth to that nasty rumor, I'd get Mr. Bishop to the nearest preacher as soon as possible. Even if the marriage ends in a few months, the marriage certificate alone would stop wagging tongues, end any speculation about your losing your job and—most importantly—ensure your child's legitimacy."

"You've got this all figured out, haven't you, Neil?" Donna positioned her face directly in front of his. "You know more than you're telling me."

Neil withdrew, pursed his lips and rose from the desk. "Marry the man, Donna. No matter how uncouth he is— and I understand he's a rounder. I've heard he was the town bad boy years ago. A *really* bad boy."

Neil smiled. Until Donna frowned at him. He cleared his throat.

"Get that marriage certificate, legitimize your daughter and then divorce the man," Neil advised. "You know as well as I do what the moral codes are in Marshallton County. We're still living in the nineteenth century around here."

"I cannot be fired simply because I'm an unwed mother!"

"No, of course not. But believe me, if the powers that be want you out, they'll find a way."

Donna shoved back her chair, stood and looked out the window behind her desk. "Thanks for stopping by, Neil. I'll keep your suggestion in mind."

"You're a smart lady. You'll do what you have to do," Neil said. "So, you made a mistake last summer. You can correct it. We all make mistakes."

Without acknowledging his comment verbally, Donna merely nodded, her silence a cue for him to leave.

"I'll talk to you later, then," he said.

When the door closed, Donna turned to find Neil gone. But his presence lingered. She couldn't afford to ignore his warnings. He was right. If Mrs. Harding and others like her, suspected that she hadn't been married to Jake, they could put a great deal of pressure on the college president and Harding would find a way to dismiss her. She could lose her job!

But was she willing to marry Jake, even briefly, to keep her position here at the college? Did she dare risk living with Jake, sharing his bed and falling in love with him?

Just as she was pondering her dilemma the phone rang. Lifting the receiver, she sighed. "Hello. Donna Fields's office."

"Oh, Donna, I'm so glad I you're there," Mrs. Winthrop said. "I just received some upsetting news."

"What is it? What's wrong?"

"My sister has suffered a heart attack. They're going to have to do a triple bypass. Eugenia lives alone in Chattanooga. I'm afraid I'll have to fly out this afternoon and it looks like I'll be gone for at least six weeks, perhaps longer.

There's no one else to take care of my sister during her recovery.''

"I'm so sorry,'' Donna said. "I'll leave immediately and come straight home.''

"I hate to leave you so abruptly. I hope you understand.''

"Yes, of course, I understand. Family comes first. Make your plans. I should be home in about fifteen minutes.''

"Thank you.''

Donna eased the receiver onto the telephone, slumped down in her swivel chair, crossed her hands behind her head and groaned. Great. Just great. This was all she needed. She had hired Mrs. Winthrop to be Louisa's nanny because she had a reputation for being the best in the area. Several acquaintances had used her before their children were old enough for play school. Where was she going to find a replacement with even half the qualifications? She absolutely refused to leave her child with someone who wasn't personally known to her.

After a moment she pulled open a bottom desk drawer, removed her purse and retrieved her keys from an inside zippered compartment. No use sitting here stewing! She got up, left her office, locked the door and headed outside to the parking lot. So much for well-laid plans. But then, what should she expect? Her life had been out of control, in one way or another, ever since she'd spent an irresponsible, passionate weekend with Jake Bishop, nine and a half months ago. All the more reason not to give in to the temptation to marry him!

Jake parked his Jeep in front of Caleb's baseball card shop in downtown Crooked Oak. He hadn't intended to stop, but when he noticed Hank's car, he decided to drop in to tell his brothers the good news. When he entered the building, he found his younger siblings in the eight-by-eight-foot office at the back. Hank sat on the edge of the desk, a coffee cup in his hand. Caleb, sitting in a leather swivel chair, had his feet propped up on the desk.

"Hey, bro." Caleb motioned for Jake to join them. "What brings you by?"

"I'm on my way over to Marshallton to see Sugar Baby," Jake said. "I go over and stay a couple of hours every night. Y'all ought to see my girl. She's growing by leaps and bounds." He smiled at the thought of his daughter. He looked forward to those two hours every evening. "I noticed your car out front, Hank, so I thought I'd stop and tell y'all that old Wayland Henry and I have made a deal for me to buy his ranch. He's retiring and moving to Birmingham to live with his daughter and son-in-law."

"How old is Mr. Henry, anyway? He must be close to a hundred," Caleb said.

"He told me he turns eighty-five next month. He wants to stay on until then, but he's instructed his lawyer to have the papers drawn up as soon as possible. The ranch should be mine within a month's time."

Hank slid off the desk, stood, and slapped Jake on the back. "Congratulations, big brother. I never thought I'd see the day you settled down."

"Yeah, well, I suppose it's past time. Besides, becoming a father changes a man's priorities. You should know that. I want to be around to see Sugar Baby grow up. I want to hear her call me Daddy. I want her to know who her old man is."

"I understand," Hank said. "Caleb and I both do. Our own father did a real number on us, didn't he? We've all been afraid of fatherhood and commitment because he was such a lousy husband and father."

"Are you going to marry Donna?" Caleb asked. "Sheila

is convinced that you two should get married as soon as possible.''

"I asked the lady to be my wife and she turned me down.''

"So, ask her again,'' Hank suggested. "Despite the fact that she's an independent woman, Donna's going to find it difficult to raise a child alone around here. People in Marshall County aren't very modern in their thinking. They expect a woman of Donna's background and social standing to be married to her child's father.''

"I think Donna's background and social standing may be one of the reasons she doesn't want to marry me. I'm afraid she doesn't think I'm good enough for her. And I can't say I blame her. After all, compared to her polish, I'm a pretty coarse guy.''

"So, you're not a cultured gentleman. Big deal,'' Caleb said. "Undoubtedly, Donna liked you well enough to have an affair with you. And from what Sheila tells me, Donna hadn't been with a man since her husband died five years ago.''

"My guess is, that even if Donna is denying she has any feelings for you, she's lying to herself as well as to you,'' Hank said. "Susan tells me that Donna was deeply in love with her husband and that when he died she nearly had a nervous breakdown. Seems it's common knowledge in Marshall County that Donna was under psychiatric care for over a year after Edward Fields died. They say her aunt and uncle were afraid she'd commit suicide.''

Jake felt a rush of jealous anger swell up inside him and fill him completely. Donna had loved her husband so much that she hadn't wanted to live without him? He wondered if part of the problem now was that Donna really was still in love with Edward. How could he compete with a dead man? The ghost of an old lover?

"I've offered her marriage," Jake said. "If she changes her mind, she'll have to let me know. But I've got to admit that the idea of competing with Donna's memory of her husband isn't my idea of a good way to start a marriage."

"Afraid of the competition?" Hank asked, a twinkle of devilment in his eyes.

"Not if the guy was flesh and blood," Jake said. "But if she's still in love with this other guy, she's going to remember him as if he were a saint. There's no way I or any other man could compete with memories of a perfect husband."

"Memories, no matter how wonderful, won't keep you warm on a cold night," Caleb said. "I'd say if you two are good in the sack together, then you have a distinct advantage over her memories of her husband."

Jake mumbled several colorful obscenities under his breath, then glanced from one brother to the other. "I'm not discussing mine and Donna's sex life with you two."

Caleb and Hank grinned, then laughed softly as if trying not to laugh at all.

"What's so damn funny?" Jake glared at his brothers.

"When a man won't talk about his sexual, er, dalliances with a particular lady, then it's usually a sure sign he's got some major feelings for the lady," Caleb said.

"Yeah," Hank agreed. "You don't happen to be in love with Donna, do you?"

The question took Jake off guard. He hadn't even thought about love. He wasn't in love with Donna, was he? He had known more than his share of women over the years and he'd truly cared about a few, but he'd never been in love. He wasn't sure he even believed in the emotion. He liked Donna. He loved making love to her. And he had feelings for her because she was the mother of his child. But love her? Nope. Jake Bishop wasn't the kind of man who went soft in the head over a woman. Any woman. Not even a special lady like Donna Fields.

"I care about her because she's Sugar Baby's mama, but that's as far as it goes—that and the fact that I want her. I think we could make marriage work, if she'd give us a chance."

"Are you going to tell her that you're buying the ranch?" Hank walked over to the coffee machine, picked up the pot and poured himself another cup.

"Don't know." Jake rubbed his chin. "She thinks I'm a penniless cowpoke who's going to have to float a major loan to buy the ranch."

"Why haven't you told her that you're a rich man?" Caleb asked.

"Maybe he doesn't want her to know that he made a lot of money as a mercenary before he retired to become cowpoke or that he's smart enough to have tripled his savings with shrewd investments." Hank looked directly at Jake. "Is that it? You want Donna to accept you, for who you are and not judge you with everyone else around here once did?"

"Yeah, something like that," Jake admitted.

Donna paced the floor, a fretful Louisa in her arms. "Hush, sweet baby, hush. Don't cry. I've fed you and changed your diaper and sung to you. What's wrong? Why won't you settle down and go to sleep? You haven't had a nap all afternoon. Mommy's just about out of her mind."

Louisa wriggled against Donna's chest and let out another yelp. Since Mrs. Winthrop had come to work as her nanny, Louisa had taken several naps every day. And when she'd been fussy, Donna and Mrs. Winthrop had taken turns caring for her. But today of all days—with Mrs. Winthrop on her way to Chattanooga and Donna having been informed her job was in jeopardy—Louisa had chosen to act her worst.

"Do you have a tummy ache?" Donna walked from her bedroom, out into the hall and down the stairs. "Maybe you need a change of scenery. Let's go downstairs and fix Mommy a bite of supper. I haven't had anything to eat since breakfast." As if on cue, Donna's stomach growled. "Listen to that! Mommy's starving."

Louisa quieted when Donna carried her into the kitchen. "Would you sit in your carrier for a few minutes so Mommy can make a sandwich?"

While the baby seemed inclined to cooperate, Donna eased her down into the carrier that was sitting in the middle of the round oak table. "That's Mommy's big girl. I promise that when I finish eating, we'll walk the floor as long as you want."

The minute Donna turned her back and headed for the cherrywood cabinets that lined the kitchen walls, Louisa bellowed. Donna halted, sighed, said a silent prayer for help and turned to face her irate infant. "We're not going to let Mommy eat, are we? Apparently, you want me to lose weight. Is that it? You think your mother needs to lose a few more pounds?"

Donna lifted Louisa into her arms, walked into the pantry and scratched around, picking up and putting down several bags as she looked for anything that might already be open. A package of cookies. Potato chips. Even rice cakes would taste delicious at this point. Donna finally gave up her search and grabbed a bag of unopened chocolate chip cookies. With one hand, she put the edge of the bag to her mouth and, using her teeth, ripped it open.

"Pay dirt," Donna said, placing the bag on the counter and delving one hand into the tattered cellophane. She retrieved a cookie, brought it to her lips and bit off a large piece. Savoring the sweetness of the cookie, she moaned with pleasure.

"Someday, my precious, you'll learn all about the healing properties of chocolate. Unfortunately, if you've inherited my fat genes, every bite of chocolate you eat will go directly to your hips."

Just as Louisa began whimpering again, the doorbell rang. Donna put the entire cookie into her mouth, chewed quickly and rushed out into the hallway. *Please, God, let it be Jake. Don't let him skip his nightly visit. Not tonight. I need him.*

Jake rang the bell again. What the hell was taking Donna so long to come to the door? She had to be home. Her Corvette was parked in the driveway. Besides, she knew he came by every night to see his daughter.

Donna flung open the front door. Jake took one look at her and stifled the laughter bubbling up in his throat. She probably had no idea how she looked. Her hair was a mess—as if she'd been caught in a high wind. Strands hung down from the untidy topknot and loosely curled about her face. Her eye makeup was smeared, her lipstick nonexistent and her blouse was buttoned crookedly. And there was a dark smear along the left corner of her mouth. Chocolate, Jake surmised.

"Thank God, you're here." Donna reached out with one hand, grabbed Jake's arm and tugged hard. "I've had the day from hell. Please, please come in."

Jake stepped into the foyer, placed his Stetson on the hall tree rack and had barely turned toward her when Donna thrust Louisa into his arms.

"Please, take her for just a few minutes! She's been throwing a temper tantrum on and off all afternoon. She hasn't had a nap and—"

"Where's Mrs. Winthrop?" Jake asked as he lifted

Louisa up against his chest. When he rubbed her back, she cooed.

"Mrs. Winthrop's sister had a heart attack. Right now, my nanny is in Chattanooga and won't be back for a couple of months, maybe longer!"

"That's too bad. I hope her sister will be all right." Jake continued to rub his daughter's back as he followed Donna into the den. "Look, sugar, why don't you let me take over for a while. You look as if you need a nice, long bubble bath—" His gaze focused on her chocolate-smeared mouth. His first thought was to lick away the stain. Instead, he reached over and wiped her mouth with the tip of his finger, then put his finger into his mouth.

"Definitely chocolate," he said.

Donna stared at him in disbelief. What had he just done? Wiped something off her mouth. Oh, good grief! She'd had chocolate from the cookie on her mouth!

"I haven't eaten a bite, except one chocolate cookie, since breakfast this morning."

Jake inclined his head toward the door. "Go upstairs, soak in a hot bath, rest, relax, and I'll take care of Sug— Louisa. And I'll take care of supper, too."

Donna nodded agreement. "Thanks, Jake. You're a life-saver! I won't be long, I promise."

"Take all the time you need. Little Miss Bishop and I will be just fine until she gets hungry again."

"I fed her about thirty minutes ago, so she should be good for another hour or two."

Donna raced out of the den. Jake sat in the recliner by the fireplace, lifted Louisa in his arms so that she faced him. "Been giving your mama a hard time today, huh?" For a split second Jake could have sworn that his daughter smiled at him. He laughed. "You're trying to show her how much you both need me, aren't you? Well, you did a good job, Sugar Baby. Your mama's nerves are frazzled. And it's to our advantage that your nanny had to go out of town.''

Louisa cooed for him, as if she understood and agreed with everything he'd said. ''You want your daddy around full-time, don't you? You don't care that your daddy has a bad boy reputation to live down or that he's not an educated gentleman. You don't even care that the thought of failing you as a father scares the hell out of me. All you care about is having me around because you know how much I love you.''

Jake got up and walked over to the desk in front of the windows overlooking the backyard. He searched the drawers for a phone book, found one, flipped through the Yellow Pages directory and memorized the number for Steak Express.

''We're going to order some supper for your mama and me. She'll be more agreeable on a full stomach.''

Jake dialed the number, placed the order and wandered through the den and out into the kitchen. He set Louisa in her carrier on the table and secured the safety belt. She didn't make a sound. He smiled down at her.

''Maybe I should find some candles and fix the table up real nice. You see, I'm going to ask your mama to marry me. Again. And this time, I'm not going to take no for an answer.''

Forty-five minutes later Donna came downstairs. Music wafted through the house, the sweet, romantic strands of guitar and piano. Jake must have turned on her CD player. She didn't hear Louisa. Was it possible that Jake had gotten her to sleep? If so, the man was a miracle worker.

When she passed the dining room on her way to the kitchen, she stopped abruptly and stared at the set table.

Two places set. China. Crystal. Silver. And candles glow-
ing brightly. Just as she took a step toward the kitchen,
Jake opened the door and walked out, his hands filled with
two large paper sacks.

"Oh, hello there," he said. "Feeling better?" He moved
past her and into the dining room.

"Where's Louisa?" Donna asked.

"Asleep in her little carrier on the kitchen table."

"You're kidding?"

"Nope. I just told her that her old man wanted a romantic dinner with her mama and she went right off to sleep."
Jake opened the sacks, removed the contents and placed
steaks and baked potatoes on the dinner plates, then filled
the bowls with salad and laid slices of cheesecake on the
dessert plates.

"I can't believe this, either. You called and had supper
delivered. Jake Bishop, you're a multitalented man."

"It's about time you realized that fact." He held out a
chair for her. "Dinner is served."

"I'm starving." She sat and gazed longingly at the filet
mignon on her plate, then up at the man who had not only
provided her with the meal, but had actually gotten their
fussy baby to take a nap.

Despite being clean-shaven, Jake's five o'clock shadow
darkened his rugged face. He was, without a doubt, the
sexiest man she'd ever known. So big, so masculine, so
irresistible. She'd be a fool to go with her instincts and ask
him to share a marriage in name only with her for the next
few months.

How would she be able to live with this man and not
succumb to him? After all, the night she met him, she'd
been mesmerized by him, so much so that she had acted
totally out of character and spent the next two days making
love with him. During the weekend they'd spent together,

he had touched every inch of her body and brought her to fulfillment countless times. Although they were still little more than strangers, Jake knew her in ways no other man ever had. Not even Edward. She'd never been a wild woman in Edward's arms, never done the things with him she'd done with Jake. Just remembering what they had shared brought a blush to Donna's cheeks.

No, she didn't dare marry Jake. It would be too dangerous. But what was the alternative to marrying him, at least on a temporary basis? Unless she could make some sort of bargain with him, she might lose her job and it was certain Louisa would suffer the stigma of illegitimacy. Something like that would have been insignificant in New York or L.A., but it still mattered in rural Tennessee.

After Jake took his seat across the table from her, Donna smiled at him. "Thank you." She sliced into her steak, then put a savory bite into her mouth.

Jake followed suit and they ate a leisurely meal, keeping the conversation light. "Nice weather. Felt like summertime today, didn't it?"

"What? Oh, yes, it was rather warm," Donna said

"Old Man Henry gave me a tour of his house today." Jake had already decided that he'd have to completely remodel the place. "Would you believe he doesn't even own an air conditioner?"

"Is that right?" Donna spread the butter around on her baked potato. "I can't imagine anyone not having air-conditioning this day and age."

"I plan to put in central heat and air when I redo the house."

"That's a good idea."

"I'd like for you to bring Louisa out to the ranch sometime, since I expect to be living there."

"Yes, of course. But there's no rush, is there? After all, you haven't bought the place yet."

"You wouldn't like living on a horse ranch, would you?"

*Of course, she wouldn't, you idiot,* taunted an inner voice. *Look around you. Donna's world is filled with every modern convenience and decorated with priceless antiques. Even if she were madly in love with you, she'd find it difficult to adjust to life on a ranch.*

"Probably not," she said. "I've lived in town all my life."

Jake nodded, then became unusually quiet. Donna knew what she had to do, but something inside her—that pesky little voice—warned her that she'd live to regret it if she allowed Louisa's father to live with them, even for a short period of time.

Jake knew it was now or never. He had to ask her—one more time. And if she rejected his proposal, he'd have to accept the fact that she wouldn't marry him and give their child two full-time parents.

"There's something I want to talk to you about," he said.

"All right, but first, there's something I want to ask you."

"What is it?"

Donna took a deep breath, then blurted, "Will you marry me?"

# Five

"Will you, Donna Deirdre Fields, take this man, James Dean Bishop, to be your lawfully wedded husband?"

Jake felt the four walls of the judge's chamber close in on him. With his brothers, their wives, their two kids and his own infant daughter surrounding him, he was trapped. He couldn't escape now, even if he wanted to. And, heaven help him, there was a big part of him that—right this minute—wanted to run like hell. Everybody knew Jake Bishop wasn't the marrying kind. He was a man who enjoyed a good time without any strings attached. And ten months ago that's just what he'd had—a mighty good time with a woman named Donna. No last names exchanged, no promises made, no hearts broken. Only thing was—this particular good time got pregnant and gave birth to his child. And as scared as he was at the prospect of even a temporary marriage, he was willing to do anything for his little girl.

"I do." Donna's voice was low and uncertain. This was

not her idea of what a wedding should be, even for a second marriage. Her wedding to Edward had been an elaborate affair in the huge Presbyterian church in Marshallton. Five hundred people had attended and enjoyed a champagne dinner at the country club afterward.

But this is a marriage in name only, she reminded herself. A marriage with a six month expiration date. She and Jake had agreed to a temporary marriage that would provide Louisa with a legitimacy that no one could question, secure Donna's position at the college and give Jake a chance to truly bond with his daughter before he became a *weekend dad.*

Donna's stomach churned, her nerves screamed and her head pounded. This was a mistake and she knew it, but she'd been unable to think of a viable alternative. And once she'd blurted her proposal to Jake, she knew he'd never let her take it back, no matter how much she had wished she could.

The ceremony was a no-frills affair, Jake thought, and was over within minutes. He was a married man!

"You may kiss the bride," Judge Randall said.

Donna turned to Jake, her cheeks flushed and her eyes bright. He knew she expected a kiss—something sedate and appropriate for the occasion. He figured he could knock her panty hose off with a real kiss, but then he'd wind up with a hard-on.

He pulled her into his arms, leaned down and gave her a soft, closemouthed kiss. His body stirred to life. Donna pressed closer. He realized that what she expected and what she wanted were two different things. Jake deepened the kiss. Donna willingly opened her mouth for his invasion. He wanted to devour her, right here and now.

The hooting and hollering from his younger brothers brought Jake to his senses. He ended the kiss, eased Donna out of his arms and smiled sheepishly when he turned to face his siblings.

Hank slapped Jake on the back. "Never thought I'd live to see the day my big brother got married."

Caleb came up on the other side, grabbed Jake's hand and shook it soundly. "Welcome to the club. Once you get used to it, you might like it. Believe it or not, Hank and I do."

Jake hadn't had the heart to tell his brothers that this marriage had a six-month shelf life and was due to be recalled by Christmas.

Susan and Sheila rushed Donna, hugged her, kissed her and whispered girlish nonsense in her ear about love and happiness and forever after. Donna cringed. She didn't like lying to her two best friends, but when she'd told them that she and Jake were getting married, they'd been so thrilled that the truth had died on her lips.

So, for all intents and purposes, the whole county—including the Bishop family—thought this marriage was a real one, meant to last a lifetime.

"I wish you'd waited long enough for us to have put together a nice wedding for you," Susan said.

"Now, Susie Q, if we'd waited for that, Big Brother might have gotten cold feet." Hank slung his arm around Jake's shoulder. "This guy's been sweating like a stuck pig for the past few days. It was better to get him hitched before he came to his senses."

Everyone laughed, including Jake, even though Donna could tell his good humor was forced. She faked a smile herself, then turned to check on Louisa, who rested on the leather sofa alongside her cousin, Lowell Bishop, both infants secure in their infant carriers. Danny stood beside the babies, watching over them, while the adults laughed and talked.

"Congratulations, Miss Donna—" Danny cleared his throat "—er…ah, I guess I should call you Aunt Donna now, huh?"

"I'd like for you to call me Aunt Donna."

"Round 'em up and head 'em out," Caleb said. "Sheila and Susan have got a little reception all set up over at Donna's place."

Jake glanced across the room at his bride. She looked back at him and smiled. He could tell the smile was as fake as their marriage. It was obvious to him that Donna was as scared and uncertain as he was. They both wanted and needed this marriage for different reasons, but his bride was far from happy about the situation. If she hadn't stipulated that there would be no sex during the duration of the marriage, they'd both have something to look forward to after her six-week checkup. He had tried to reason with her, to make her see how foolish it was for them not to enjoy the one thing they had in common, other than their child. But she'd been adamant that she didn't want to have sex with him. Ever again! He had agreed, but with his own stipulation—that they sleep in the same bed together. She had accepted his request, reluctantly.

Jake walked over, lifted Louisa's carrier and slipped his arm around Donna's waist. She looked beautiful today. Good enough to eat with a spoon, and that's just what he'd like to do. The pale green suit she wore was very simple, but elegant, like the lady herself. Susan had pinned a small gardenia corsage on the lapel of the suit. The flowers, plus the diamond and pearl earrings Donna wore, were her only decoration.

The gold bands they had exchanged were real enough, but inexpensive when compared to Donna's other jewelry. He could have bought her a big diamond, but if he had, she'd have figured out he wasn't the penniless cowpoke she thought he was. And despite Hank's and Caleb's warnings not to keep secrets from his new wife, Jake's stubborn male pride wouldn't let him reveal the truth about his finances. If Donna accepted him, she'd have to do it thinking he didn't have a dime to his name.

"Let's go home, sugar," Jake said.

Donna put Louisa in her basinet, kicked off her heels and padded across the floor to the bathroom. This had been the longest day of her life! She had appreciated the lovely reception Susan and Sheila had prepared for them, but was glad Jake's family had left and she no longer had to pretend to be the joyful June bride.

She removed her clothes, slipped into her gown, robe and slippers, then loosened her hair from the French twist and brushed it with her fingers.

This was her wedding night, but there would be no honeymoon, no making love all night. Her body tightened and released, sending a quivering sensation through her femininity. Her body remembered the pleasure of Jake's possession, the ecstasy of his touch.

"I can't!" she told her traitorous body. "When he makes love to me, I can't think straight. I lose my good sense." She stared at herself in the mirror. *You are not going to give in to him. Do you hear me! You are not going to care about this man. You are not going to fall in love with him.*

She heard Jake enter her bedroom. *Their* bedroom, now. She took a deep breath, squared her shoulders and opened the bathroom door. She stopped dead in her tracks when she saw Jake standing there in nothing but his briefs. He was the most magnificent male specimen she'd ever seen. Tall, broad-shouldered, long-legged, slim-hipped and muscular. His dark olive complexion had tanned, giving his skin a golden bronze sheen.

She stood there, watching him as he lifted his suitcase to the bed, unzipped it and removed a pair of jeans and athletic shoes. Just as he slid the jeans over his hips, he cocked his head to one side and glanced toward the bathroom.

"Hello there." He grinned.

The bottom dropped out of her stomach. *Don't you grin at me!* she wanted to scream. *When you smile at me that way, I go weak in the knees.*

"I fixed you a plate. I'll get it for you when we go back downstairs," he said, tugging on his shoes. "I noticed you didn't eat much at our reception. I thought you might be hungry."

"Did it ever occur to you that I might be trying to cut back, not eat so much, so I can lose a little of this *baby* fat I put on during my pregnancy?" Donna realized she had practically taken off his head, but she couldn't bear it when he was so damn nice to her.

"You look fine to me, sugar." He took a T-shirt out of his suitcase, pulled it over his head and stuffed the bottom into his unzipped jeans. "Besides, you can't expect to drop all your *baby* fat in just four weeks."

When she didn't respond or move from the doorway, Jake strolled over to her, took her hand and pulled her out into the room. "We're going downstairs and you will eat something, even if I have to spoon-feed you, myself."

He tugged on her hand. She hesitated, then followed his lead, but halted suddenly in the middle of the room. "Get the baby monitor," she said. "Louisa probably won't sleep more than an hour before she'll want to be fed. She has a big appetite for such a young baby."

"She's a big girl with a big appetite, just like her daddy's."

"Well, if I'm honest, I have a pretty big appetite myself." Donna sighed as she glanced down at her round hips.

"Yeah, I know." Jake looked directly at Donna's parted lips. "That's one of the things I like about you—your appetite."

Donna averted her gaze, not wanting Jake to see the realization in her eyes. She knew perfectly well what kind of appetite he meant. She'd been shameless during their weekend together—insatiable in her hunger for him.

Jake retrieved the baby monitor from the nightstand, slipped his arm around Donna's waist and led her out into the hall and down the stairs.

They raided the kitchen, then Donna curled up in the recliner in the den, a plate of edible delights in her lap. Jake stretched out on the hunter green corduroy sofa, a beer in his hand. The thought went through Donna's mind that they were acting like an old married couple instead of a bride and groom on their wedding night. She sighed softly.

"Caleb is pretty excited about Sheila being pregnant," Jake said.

"What? Oh, yes, he is." Donna nibbled on the cucumber sandwich.

"He missed her pregnancy with Danny and all those years with his son." Jake took a swig from the beer bottle. "I'm sorry I wasn't around while you were pregnant, but luckily, I'm here now, so I won't miss Sug—Louisa's babyhood."

"I'm sorry that I didn't try to find you to let you know I was pregnant." Donna shifted in the coral-and-green-plaid recliner, so that she had a better view of Jake. "I honestly didn't think you'd want to know…that you'd care."

"Yeah, well…why should you? After all, we didn't really know each other. You just assumed I was a horny cowboy out for a good time."

"And you weren't?" she asked teasingly.

Jake laughed. "Yeah, you're right. I was. But there's more to me than that. I admit that I deserved my reputation as a bad boy here in Marshall County, and for years after I left Tennessee. But I'm thirty-six and I've slowed down a little." He took another gulp of beer. "Besides, I've never been a father before and I find I take that responsibility very seriously."

"I've noticed." Donna finished off one tiny sandwich, then lifted another to her mouth. "By the way, just what did you do all those years after you left Tennessee? I know you were a cowboy when I met you last summer. How long had you been working on a ranch?"

Jake took a deep breath, then let it out slowly. "I guess it is time you and I got to know each other a little better, isn't it? After all, we're married now, and married folks should be a lot better acquainted than you and I are."

"Do you mind talking about your past?"

"Nope. Do you?"

"I'm afraid my life has probably been pretty dull compared to yours."

Jake chuckled, finished off his beer and set it on a coaster on the coffee table. Then he stretched out on the sofa. Twining his fingers together, he placed his hands behind his head. "Where should I start?"

"At the beginning," she suggested. "When you first left Crooked Oak."

"That was a long time ago. I was eighteen and had dropped out of high school a year before to work on a neighbor's farm."

"You didn't like farming?"

"I liked farming just fine." Jake hadn't thought about that long-ago summer for years. It had been a time in his life he preferred to forget. "Let's just say the man I worked for and I had a serious difference of opinion and he gave me a choice—leave town or he'd press charges and I'd wind up spending a few years in the pen.''

Donna choked on a bite of mini quiche. Coughing several times, she cleared her throat. "Did I hear you right?"

"Yeah, but it's not what you think. He accused me of stealing some money, but I hadn't stolen anything. What I'd done was attract his young wife. She made a play for me and I thought I was doing the right thing by rejecting her.''

"What did she do, tell her husband that you'd come on to her?"

"Yeah, something like that. I think Mr. Acklin knew his wife well enough to suspect the truth, but he had to find a way to get rid of me.''

"Where did you go? What did you do?"

"I picked up odd jobs and worked my way across the country.''

Jake wondered just how much he should tell Donna. Not everything. Not by a long shot. He'd done some things he'd rather she never know about and a few things he wasn't too proud of. "When I was nineteen, I hooked up with some guys who did jobs out of the country. Jobs that paid well.''

"What sort of jobs?"

"Dirty jobs, sometimes illegal jobs. These guys were mercenaries, sugar. I was a crack shot from having hunted since I was a kid and I was a hell-raiser, a bit cocky and full of the devil. At first, I thought being a hired soldier was exciting. And the money was great.''

He wasn't going to tell his bride that he had saved a great deal of that money or that in his early thirties, he'd chosen investments that had, within the past couple of years, made him a wealthy man. A man rich enough to buy his own ranch and have plenty left over.

"How long were you a...a mercenary?" Just thinking about the kind of life he'd once lived sent a shiver through Donna. Had Jake actually been a solider for hire, a man who sold his services to the highest bidder?

"I lived dangerously, loved it, got paid well, used that money to enjoy the high life. By the time I was thirty, I'd had enough." He intentionally left out the really bad parts of his life and the real reason he'd given up the soldier of fortune business. He'd been on the verge of losing what humanity 'he'd had left. He'd almost become an unfeeling machine.

"Is that when you became a cowboy?" Donna picked up the glass of skim milk and sipped. She didn't like milk, but as long as she was nursing Louisa, she'd have to drink several glasses a day.

"I sort of fell into life as a ranch hand," Jake said. "I was bumming around the southwest, met up with some guys in a bar who said their boss was looking for another hand." Donna didn't need to know that he'd been drunk, gotten into a fight over a bosomy blonde and wound up putting two guys in the hospital. His newfound friends had bailed him out of jail and testified in his defense.

"I'd never been in a bar—the honky-tonk kind of bar—until the night I meet you at the Blue Bonnet Grill," Donna admitted. "Joanie talked me into trying something different."

Jake lifted himself up until his head rested on the cushioned arm of the sofa, then turned sideways and glanced over at Donna. "I'm glad you took a walk on the wild side. If you hadn't, we wouldn't have Louisa. And you know what? Despite the circumstances, I'm getting to like the idea of being a father." He chuckled when he saw the questioning look in Donna's eyes. "Yeah, well, of course, I'm still scared spitless that I might turn out to be a real dud as a father."

"Edward and I had planned to have two children." Donna closed her eyes and tried to picture Edward's face—the kind, gentle face that she had loved. The image was fuzzy in her mind, like a faded photograph. Suddenly the image changed, Edward's face disappeared and was replaced by the strong, chiseled features of Jake Bishop. Her eyelids flew open. She gasped audibly.

"You're still in love with him, aren't you? Even after all these years, he's still the man you want." Jake sat up, ran his fingers through his hair and stood. "I think I'll get myself another beer."

"Jake?"

He hesitated momentarily. "Yeah?"

"I want you to know that I wasn't thinking about Edward during the weekend I spent with you. I didn't use you as a substitute for him."

"Thanks for telling me." Jake's tense shoulders relaxed. "Want anything else while I'm in the kitchen?"

"Would you mind taking this tray? I've finished."

Jake took the tray from her. When his hand accidentally brushed hers, their gazes locked and held. Jake leaned closer, his mouth a hair breadth from hers.

Donna's heartbeat accelerated. He was going to kiss her. *Yes! Please, Jake, kiss me.*

Louisa whimpered. The sound came through the baby monitor loud and clear. Jake and Donna paused. Louisa began crying, softly at first and then suddenly she screamed. Jake kissed Donna's forehead.

"Our little princess is calling," he said. "Want me to get her?"

"No, I'll get her. I imagine she's hungry again." Donna

handed Jake the tray, then stood. "I'll bring her down here, after I change her diaper."

"Would you like for me to put on a pot of decaf coffee? I could have a cup waiting for you."

"That sounds wonderful. Thanks."

Jake headed for the kitchen. He supposed it was a good thing Sugar Baby interrupted before he could kiss Donna. He'd wanted a lot more than a kiss and he knew his bride wasn't ready for more. Neither physically nor emotionally.

He took his time in the kitchen, cleaning up and preparing their coffee. Fifteen minutes later, he checked in the den and found Donna resting in the big recliner, Louisa at her breast. He stepped inside far enough so that Donna saw him.

"Do you want coffee now?" He mouthed the words in a low whisper.

She nodded that she did, so he returned to the kitchen and came back with a travel mug of rich gourmet coffee in one hand and a beer bottle in the other. He set the covered mug down on the wine table beside the chair. Donna reached out, put the mug to her lips and sipped.

Holding the mug in one hand, she sighed. "This is great. Another talent you have, Mr. Bishop—making superb coffee."

"Thanks for noticing," he said as he sat on the sofa. He held the beer bottle between his legs. "By the way, I appreciate your saying what you did—about that weekend we spent together. I'm glad to know that I was the man you wanted and I wasn't a stand-in for your late husband."

"Edward was the only man I've ever loved…the only man I'll ever love." *I can't love you, Jake. Not you or anyone else. Loving and losing is far too painful. I will never put myself through that kind of agony again.*

"Yeah, you've made that abundantly clear." Jake lifted the bottle to his lips and downed half the beer.

"I'm sorry, I... We did the right thing today, didn't we? I mean, we both get what we want out of this marriage. You get a chance to bond with Louisa, to be a full-time father to her for six months. And I have a marriage certificate to wave around if anyone questions my daughter's legitimacy."

"Yeah, sure. We both get what we want." Jake finished off the beer. "Will it bother Louisa if I watch a little TV?"

"No, I don't think so, as long as you keep the volume down."

Jake picked up the remote, flipped through the channels and then paused on a sports network. A baseball game. Yeah, sure, they both got what they wanted. Like hell they did! What he really wanted was a wedding night, something along the lines of the weekend they'd shared last summer.

*And what Donna really wants is Edward Fields!* mocked that infernal inner voice.

Donna sang softly to Louisa as the child nursed. She would never regret her affair with Jake because her precious baby had been conceived during that torrid weekend. Having a child was worth the price she'd had to pay—and was still paying. She wanted to believe that Jake would get something out of this marriage, but she knew she was the true beneficiary of today's wedding. In six months Jake would become a part-time father, with only visitation rights.

"Has Mr. Henry named a price for his ranch?" Donna asked, her voice low so she wouldn't disturb Louisa.

"Yeah, he named a price."

"Do you think you'll have a problem getting a loan?"

"Why do you ask?"

"Well, I was thinking about things—you know, the fact

that you're doing me a big favor by marrying me and pretending to be my real husband and—''

"I am your real husband," Jake said.

"You know what I mean. Anyway, I'm a fairly wealthy woman and I thought perhaps I could loan you the money to buy Mr. Henry's ranch. You could pay me back when you started making a profit."

Jake sat there on the sofa and stared at her. His gaze narrowed until all she saw were two slits instead of his eyes.

"Thanks for the offer, but I'll handle the financial arrangements for buying the ranch. I married you for Louisa's sake. You don't owe me a thing."

Donna felt as if he'd slapped her. Her eyes blinked. Her heart pounded. She tried to smile, but the effort produced a sickly little grin that vanished quickly. He's a proud man, she told herself. He might be poor, but he didn't want her charity. That wasn't what he'd said, but his irate look conveyed his feelings quite adequately.

She turned her attention to her baby. The child's small head was moist with perspiration. Donna stroked the silky black strands of Louisa's hair. Hair the color of Jake's. She glanced over at her child's father, but he seemed absorbed in the baseball game on television. She closed her eyes, leaned her head back and tried to erase everything from her mind. Especially the sight of the big man lounging on her sofa.

Jake almost nodded off to sleep. He'd had two beers and a long, difficult day. His wedding day. What a joke! He glanced over at Donna. Her eyes were closed. He wondered if she was asleep. Louisa lay in her arms, sleeping peacefully, her rosy cheek resting against Donna's bare breast. At the sight of that full, round breast, Jake's sex hardened.

Hell, he couldn't even look at the woman without wanting her.

"Donna?"

She didn't move, didn't respond in any way.

He got up, walked over and touched her arm. She sighed. Realizing she was sleeping as soundly as their daughter, he decided that they'd both sleep better upstairs in their beds. He eased his hand under Louisa, lifted her away from Donna and tiptoed out of the room. He went upstairs, placed Louisa in her crib, then returned downstairs to the den.

He debated whether or not to awaken his sleeping bride. Dear God, she was so damn pretty! Unable to resist the urge to touch her, he ran the tip of his index finger over her exposed nipple. A drop of milk trickled out. He sucked in a deep breath and hurriedly pulled up and closed the flap on her nursing bra. Then he lifted her into his arms. She murmured something unintelligible and cuddled against his chest. Heaven help him! He was hard and hurting and she was cuddling her soft body against him.

Jake carried her upstairs to her bedroom—their bedroom. Reaching down with one hand, he jerked the covers back and slid her onto the bed. He slipped off her robe and tossed it to the foot of the bed. She stretched, turned over and hugged her pillow.

What he needed was a cold shower! He went into the bathroom, stripped down and turned on the water faucets. Five minutes later, shaking like a leaf, he got out, dried off and put on a clean pair of briefs. When he went back into the bedroom, he noticed that Donna had kicked off all the cover and lay there with her gown hiked up, revealing her shapely thighs.

*Just get in the damn bed and go to sleep! Don't look at her. And whatever you do, don't touch her again!*

Jake lay down, pulled the covers up over them and stayed as far to his side of the bed as possible. He lay there, looking up at the ceiling, telling himself that he could survive this night—and all the nights ahead of him. Donna had suggested they sleep apart, but he'd been determined to win this one battle. He had foolishly thought that if they shared a bed, sooner or later, she'd want him again.

He didn't know how long he lay there listening to the sound of her breathing—thirty minutes or three hours. Suddenly, without warning, Donna turned toward him, stretched out her arm and draped it across his chest. Her fingers caressed him, then spread out through his curly chest hair.

Oh, man! This wasn't fair. He'd been careful not to touch her and now here she was reaching out to him in her sleep. But did she know who she was touching? Did she think she was caressing her beloved Edward?

Jake removed her arm, laid it at her side, then turned his back to her. She rolled over against him, spoon fashion, and cuddled her warm, soft curves against his hard, tense back. She threw her arm around his waist and rested her hand on his belly.

Oh, yeah, he was going to get a lot of sleep tonight! If he didn't like the feel of her against him so much, he'd get up and go to another bedroom.

*You're a glutton for punishment, Bishop. You'd rather lay here and suffer with a rock-solid hard-on than give up the pleasure of having her wrapped around you like this.*

Sometime before dawn, Jake finally dozed off to sleep. Exhausted. Frustrated. And blatantly aroused.

# Six

Jake sat at the kitchen table, talking typical parental nonsense to his six-week-old daughter. Louisa smiled a big toothless grin at her father. Donna had explained that at this stage in her development, Louisa would smile at anyone who looked into her eyes or even at large objects held close to her face. However, Jake preferred to think his daughter recognized him.

"Yeah, Daddy's sugar baby is the best girl in the whole wide world, isn't she?" he crooned to her. "And the prettiest and the smartest and—"

"And she's being terribly spoiled by her daddy," Donna said as she walked into the kitchen.

"Good morning." Jake looked at his wife, who had come down for breakfast in her gown. During the past few weeks she had begun to relax around him, as he had her. They were getting used to living together. Except for the fact that they didn't have sex, their marriage seemed fairly

normal. "Coffee's ready." He nodded toward the two cof-
feemakers—one for her decaf and a second for his regular
brew.

"Thanks." She glanced at the electric skillet on the
counter. "Have you already had breakfast?"

"Nope, Sugar Baby...sorry, I mean, Louisa and I were
waiting for Mommy, weren't we?" He leaned down and
rubbed his nose across his baby girl's. She gurgled and
gooed. "I fixed pancake batter and thought I'd whip us up
some."

"Jake, you're incredible, you know that?" Donna poured
herself a cup of coffee and sat at the table. Leaning over,
she kissed Louisa's forehead. "Your daddy had to work
late last night and yet here he is up with you, and has not
only already made coffee, but he's made pancake batter."

"We aim to please." Jake opened the refrigerator door,
removed a large glass bowl and placed it on the countertop.
"How many do you want?" he asked as he took a large
spoon and stirred the mixture.

"Oh, gee, I'd love three, but I really don't need that
many. What with syrup and butter, the calories will add up.
I should eat one, but maybe I'll splurge and have two."

"Splurging is eating three pancakes," Jake said. "You
can have two without any guilt." His gaze examined her
quickly, from head to toe. "Besides, I don't see why you're
so worried about a few extra pounds. You just gave birth
six weeks ago. And I kind of like where most of that extra
weight is located." He gazed meaningfully at her breasts.

She rolled up a place mat, jumped up, flew across the
kitchen and swatted Jake repeatedly. He cringed in mock
fear, held up his hands to ward off her attack and cried out
his apology. As they playacted their fight, they both
laughed. Within minutes Jake slipped his arms around her
and brought her body close to his. Her breasts rubbed

against his chest. She threw her arms around his neck and gazed into his eyes. He cupped her buttocks, lifted her up and pressed her into his arousal.

She pulled away from him and stepped back, then took a deep, calming breath. "Fix the pancakes. Only two. Contrary to your male observation of the weight distribution, I know for a fact that most of my weight gain is below my waist."

"Whatever you want," he said as he set the thermometer on the skillet. "Guess sausage links are not on the menu, huh?"

"God forbid!" Donna was grateful that Jake had returned to his playful attitude. She wasn't sure how she would have handled the situation between them these past few weeks if he hadn't been a perfect gentleman. Whenever things became intense between them, she had managed to back off just in time—and Jake had never pushed for more than she'd been willing to give.

Louisa let out a shrill cry. Jake and Donna rushed over to the infant carrier. The moment the adults came into her line of vision, she whimpered, then cooed.

"Looks like somebody thought she was being ignored." Jake gently placed his big hand over his daughter's round little tummy. "You're the center of attention now, Sugar Baby." Glancing at Donna, he shrugged. "Sorry, but it's difficult for me not to call her that. I keep trying to call her Louisa all the time, but the other just slips out."

"It's all right," Donna said. "I suppose there are worse nicknames than Sugar Baby."

"You do realize that even when she's eighteen and has a dozen boyfriends, I'll still think of her as my sugar baby."

Donna stared at Jake as he walked over to the counter. With his back to her, his broad shoulders looked five feet

wide. Her stomach did a crazy flip-flop. Why did the man
have to be so physically attractive and why had he turned
out to be such a caring father? Keeping him at arm's length
would be so much easier if she didn't like him. But she
did like him—liked him far too much.

"You really intend to be around when she's eighteen,
don't you?"

Jake tested the skillet by tossing a few drops of water on
the heated surface, then poured the pancake batter into circles. "What did you think, that I'd lose interest in my
daughter after our divorce?"

"I suppose that's what I thought at first, but…I'm sorry.
I know you've made a commitment to Louisa. It's just that
you didn't seem like the type of man who would want to
be a father, let alone actually be happy about having a
daughter."

Jake flipped the pancakes. "To be honest, you had me
pegged right. I never wanted to be a father. My old man
was a lousy example. And my grandfather, who raised us,
did his best, but he was a cold, stern man who got stuck
with his son's four kids. Kids he took because nobody else
wanted us.

"I've never been interested in getting married and having kids. I figured I'd die a crusty old bachelor, but when
the thought crossed my mind about children, I saw myself
with a son. A hard-ass like me doesn't know the first thing
about little girls. Tallie was the biggest tomboy around. We
usually forgot she was a girl."

"You didn't seem the least bit disappointed that Louisa
was a girl."

Jake lifted the pancakes onto two plates, picked up the
plates and carried them to the table. "Your breakfast, ma-
dam." He set her food down in front of her. "As far as
Louisa being a girl, I was surprised—by the fact that you

were pregnant and by our child being female. Shook me up pretty bad at first.''

"And now?'' Donna spread butter over the pancakes, then doused them with a generous serving of maple syrup.

"Now, I'm still intimidated by the fact that I have a daughter. I realize more and more every day what a tremendous responsibility raising a child will be, but...well, I can't imagine my life now without Louisa in it." *Or without you,* he thought. He wanted mother and daughter to be a package deal.

"I'm sorry that I was so stubborn about your being a part of her life,'' Donna said. "I promise that we'll work out generous visitation rights.''

"How about we practice those visitation rights starting tomorrow?''

Donna raised her fork, sliced off a piece of pancake and lifted it to her mouth. "What do you mean?''

"You're supposed to go to the doctor for your six-week checkup tomorrow, aren't you?''

"Yes.'' Donna put the food in her mouth and chewed slowly, savoring the buttery-sweet goodness.

"How about letting me take Louisa out to the ranch with me, while you're at the doctor's office? I could take off a few hours from work. The boss won't mind. He's a sucker for kids.'' Jake grinned. He wasn't ready to tell her—not yet—that he was his own boss. "I'd like my daughter to become familiar with the ranch. After all, it's where I'll be living and it'll be her home, too. At least, part-time.''

Donna swallowed the food in her mouth, cleared her throat and smiled at Jake. "That's a nice idea, but I've already arranged for a baby-sitter.''

"Who?''

"One of my former students. A very reliable young

woman named Lindsay Crabtree. You don't have a problem
with that, do you?''

"No problem,'' he said. "It's just that you didn't mention it before.''

"I contacted Lindsay and as luck would have it, she's
available all summer, so I may hire her to come in several
hours every day, to help out. You know I haven't had any
luck finding a new nanny and I'll have to find someone
before mid-August when I have to go back to work at the
college.''

"You could take off another quarter and not go back to
teaching until after Christmas. After all, it's not as if you
need the money.''

"Under normal circumstances, that's just what I'd do,
but since our marriage isn't a real one and you're not in a
financial position to help me, I think it best for me to go
back to work in the fall.''

"What makes you think I can't help you out financially?
I do plan to pay child support.''

"I understand your wanting to take your responsibilities
seriously. But I thought, since I'm in much better financial
shape than you are, we could forego the child support, until
you start making a profit out at the ranch.''

"You let me worry about my money,'' Jake said. "If
you want to stay home with Louisa until after Christmas,
then stay home with her.''

Donna stared at Jake, puzzled by his comment and the
fierceness of his response. Had she touched a sore spot
mentioning money matters? She had come to realize that
he was a proud man. Perhaps he didn't want to admit he
couldn't afford to support his daughter.

"I suppose I can afford to stay home with Louisa until
after Christmas.'' She reached over and laid her hand on
Jake's arm. "I'm a fairly wealthy woman. I certainly have

enough money to support myself and Louisa for six months, without my salary from the college. And I wasn't implying that you couldn't pay child support after we're divorced. I simply want you to know that I don't need any money from you.''

"It seems you don't need much of anything from me." Jake jerked his arm away from her touch, scooted back his chair and stood. "Leave the dishes. I'll clean them up when I get back."

"Where are you going?"

"Out," he said. "I need some fresh air to clear my head."

She wanted to say something that would stop him from leaving, but what could she say? Obviously, she had offended him, even angered him. She was sorry if she'd bruised his male ego, but she was just trying to ease some of the financial burden on him.

"Your father is not only a proud man, he's stubborn." Donna leaned over the infant carrier and gazed down into her daughter's brown eyes.

Louisa Christine Bishop might have inherited her mother's soft femininity, which rounded the sharp features she had inherited from Jake but in every aspect, she was her father's daughter. Her jet black hair, her dark eyes, her olive skin. A square, stubborn jaw and even the curve of her wide mouth were replicas of the man who had just stormed out of the kitchen.

"You're very beautiful, you know," Donna said. "And when you're eighteen, your father will have to beat the boys off with a stick." Donna laughed. "Actually, he won't need to use a stick. All he'll have to do is give the boys one of his hard, stern looks and they'll run for their lives. You may be thirty before you have a date, you know. Whenever a boy comes over, your daddy will open the front door and scare the heck out of him.''

Suddenly Donna realized that she envisioned a future with Jake, a life that included him living in the same house with her and Louisa. *Don't do this to yourself. Don't let your heart make plans involving Jake Bishop. You don't love him, no matter how much you want him. You cannot love him. Not now. Not ever.*

''So, what did he say?'' Sheila asked when Donna emerged from the OB-GYN's office into the waiting area. ''Did he give you the green light for a real honeymoon?''

Donna forced a smile. Neither she nor Jake had told his family that their marriage was a short-term deal. They all seemed so happy that Donna had joined the Bishop clan that she and Jake had decided to wait awhile before explaining the situation.

''Clean bill of health,'' Donna said. ''I'm in amazing physical shape for a woman who just had a baby. As a matter of fact, Dr. Farr said that he'd never seen a woman recover so quickly from childbirth.''

''It's those birthing hips of yours,'' Sheila teased. ''I've got them, too.''

Donna checked her watch. ''I can't believe I didn't have to wait an hour or two to get in today.''

''We're lucky that Dr. Farr wasn't backed up this morning,'' Sheila said as she and Donna left the doctor's office. ''Since we got out so early, why don't we take advantage of the extra time and go out for lunch?''

''I don't know. This is the first time I've left Louisa with someone other than Jake or Mrs. Winthrop.''

''Give Lindsay a call and check on Louisa, then let's head over to the Box Lunch and devour something fattening and delicious.''

"Okay," Donna agreed. "I'll call Lindsay, then meet you at the restaurant."

Donna slid behind the wheel of her Corvette, retrieved her cellular phone from her purse and tossed the leather bag on the passenger seat. She punched the call button and waited for the ring.

"Hello. Bishop residence," Lindsay said.

"Hi, Lindsay. I finished up at Dr. Farr's early and I thought I'd join my sister-in-law for lunch. How is Louisa? Do you need me to come home?"

"Take as long as you want, Ms. Fields…er, I mean, Mrs. Bishop. Louisa's been a perfect angel."

"All right. I should be home in an hour. You've got my cell number, if you need me."

"Yes, ma'am."

When Donna arrived at the Box Lunch, Sheila waved at her from the back of the crowded restaurant, where she had secured them a booth by the windows.

After Donna slid into the booth, Sheila handed her a menu. "The special today is Rubens, with curly fries. And they have strawberry shortcake for dessert."

"You can afford to eat anything you want this early in your pregnancy," Donna said. "But I'm trying to get rid of fifteen extra pounds that have settled around my bottom."

Sheila glanced at Donna's bosom. "I don't think it all settled around your bottom."

"That's what Jake said." Donna realized, too late, that her comment had implied an intimacy in her relationship with Jake. "I didn't mean that the way it sounded. Jake and I were discussing my weight gain and—"

"Honey, you don't need to feel embarrassed. After all, Jake is your husband."

"I suppose I'm not used to the idea, yet."

"You'll get used to it. By the time you celebrate your first anniversary, you'll wonder how you ever lived without him."

"That's the way you feel about Caleb, isn't it?"

"Yes, of course." Sheila blushed. "Being Caleb's wife and having his children is all I've ever wanted."

Donna envied her friend—her sister-in-law. Donna had loved Edward with all her heart and when he'd died, she had longed to die, too. It had taken a year of therapy for her to overcome the unhealthy grief that put suicidal thoughts in her mind. Edward's death had robbed her not only of the love of her life, but it had also almost taken away her sanity. She would not allow herself to be in that position again. No man would ever mean that much to her.

"Let's order." Donna lifted the menu. "I'm going to get the Ruben and the fries, but I'll leave the shortcake alone."

Thirty-five minutes later, the waitress handed each of them a fork, then set the huge strawberry shortcake between them.

"Enjoy, ladies," the waitress said.

"I'll regret this when I weigh myself again." Donna sliced into the delectable dessert. "But right now, I just don't care."

Sheila joined her and the two of them moaned with pleasure as they shared the sinfully rich delight. Just as Donna wiped her mouth and reached for her coffee cup, her cellular phone rang.

Her heart caught in her throat. Louisa. Something was wrong with Louisa. She knew instinctively.

She grabbled in her purse, pulled out the phone and answered the ring. "Hello?"

"Oh, Mrs. Bishop, you've got to come home right now."

"What's wrong, Lindsay?" Donna's heartbeat drummed in her ears.

"I don't know. I gave Louisa her bottle and she went to sleep, but she woke up a few minutes ago and started vomiting."

"I'll be right home," Donna said. "Call Dr. Nelson and tell him that I'll bring Louisa straight to his office."

"I'm so sorry, Mrs. Bishop. I don't know what happened. She was fine and then suddenly she was sick."

"Try to stay calm. Call Dr. Nelson. Tell him Louisa's symptoms. I'll be home immediately." Donna tossed the phone into her purse, scooted out of the booth and stood.

"I'll follow you in my car," Sheila said.

"First, please, get in touch with Jake and tell him to meet me at Dr. Nelson's office. I think Jake said something about going to the sale barn today. He may be over in Colville."

"If he isn't at the ranch, I'll have Caleb run over to Colville. You go on home and get Louisa to the doctor. We'll find Jake and let him know you need him."

Donna rushed out of the restaurant, raced home at record speed and dashed into her house. All the while, she kept considering the worst possibilities—every horrible thing conceivable. What if Louisa was dying? Oh, God! She wanted Jake. She needed him desperately.

Lindsay met Donna at the front door, a screaming Louisa in her arms. Tears streamed down the young woman's face. "She's so sick. She's been throwing up for the past fifteen minutes."

"Did you call Dr. Nelson?"

"Yes, and he said bring her right in to the office."

Donna broke every speed record on the way to the pediatric clinic. The nurse met them the moment they arrived and showed them straight into an examining room. No sooner had Donna entered the room with Louisa in her arms, than Dr. Nelson walked in.

''Now, let's see what's wrong with little Miss Bishop,'' he said.

Jake couldn't keep his mind on the horseflesh being paraded in front of him. Good thing he hadn't come to buy or sell today. He'd driven over to Colville to the sale barn in hopes of running away from his anger. He had planned the morning as an outing for himself and Louisa—his daughter's first trip to his ranch. But Donna had made other plans. He supposed he'd better get used to the idea that Donna would be the one making most of the plans for Louisa's life, and that she probably wasn't going to consult him before she made the decisions.

He and his soon-to-be ex-wife would have to come to an understanding about their child. He hadn't planned on fatherhood, but now that it had been thrust on him, he wasn't about to turn his back on Sugar Baby and become an absentee father. He wanted to be a full-time dad, but Donna wasn't willing to try to make their marriage work.

Jake wanted his daughter to know him, to spend part of her time at the ranch, learning about horses. He'd get her a pony when she was a little older and he'd teach her to ride. He could picture her now, her black hair flying in the wind, as they rode together out over the ranch. He wanted their times together to be perfect. Fun times. Moments his little girl would remember all her life.

The auctioneer rattled off a description of the roan mare being led out to the front. Jake looked her over, dismissed her and glanced around the sale barn. The guy entering the building looked like Caleb. Hell, it was Caleb. What was his brother doing here?

Jake noticed Caleb searching the crowd. His baby brother must be looking for him. An odd sensation hit him in the pit of his stomach. Something was wrong. Something had happened to Louisa! He knew it in his gut.

Jake made his way toward the entrance and met Caleb. "What's wrong?"

"Dammit, man, you've got to get yourself a cell phone!" Caleb grabbed Jake's arm. "It's Louisa. Donna has rushed her to the doctor. She's sick. Vomiting and diarrhea. Donna's in a panic. Sheila sent me to get you and she drove on over to Dr. Nelson's office."

A cold, sick feeling spread from Jake's belly through his whole body. If anything happened to his sugar baby, he— None of that! Don't even consider the worst. Babies get sick all the time. It's usually nothing! But his baby girl didn't get sick every day. She'd been extremely healthy since the moment she was born.

"Where's this doctor's office?" Jake asked as he and Caleb headed for the parking area.

"The pediatric clinic in Marshallton, down on State Street. You can follow me. I'll take you straight to it."

"Thanks."

Jake was surprised that neither he nor Caleb were stopped for speeding. They'd driven like madmen to reach the clinic. Jake didn't wait for Caleb to park and get out before he leaped out of his Jeep and stormed into the doctor's office. The waiting area was filled with mothers and children of various ages, sizes and colors.

"Where's my daughter?" Jake demanded as he shoved open the only door leading to the examining rooms.

The receptionist called out to him. "Sir, you can't go back there!"

Jake paused, glanced over his shoulder and said, "I'm Jake Bishop. My wife rushed my daughter in here about thirty minutes ago. Where are they?"

"In Room Three, Mr. Bishop," she replied. "Go right on back."

Jake marched down the hallway, flung open the door to Room Three and saw a short, slender young man in a white coat holding a very pale Louisa. His heart stopped for a split second.

"Oh, Jake!" Donna cried and ran toward him.

Her eyes were red and swollen. He opened his arms and took her into his embrace. "I'm here, sugar. I'm here." As he stroked her back, he leaned down and kissed her forehead, then grasped her chin between his thumb and index finger. Lifting her face, he asked, "What's wrong with Louisa?"

Donna clung to him, gulping, sobbing. After clearing her throat, she tried to speak. "She was…so sick. I was scared to death. Oh, Jake…she's…" She choked on another sob.

"Your daughter will be fine, Mr. Bishop," Dr. Nelson said. "You and your wife can take her home now."

"Sugar Baby's fine?" Keeping one arm secured around Donna's waist, he turned to the pediatrician. "What happened? What was wrong with her? Caleb said she was vomiting and had diarrhea."

Dr. Nelson laid Louisa in Donna's arms. "Here, Mommy, I know you want to hold her."

Donna spread kisses all over her baby's tiny head. "You mustn't ever get sick again and scare your mama like that. Do you hear me?"

The doctor chuckled. "Mr. Bishop, the baby-sitter gave your little Louisa a bottle of formula, after Louisa had taken all the breast milk your wife had left for her. And it just so happened that that particular formula didn't agree with Louisa. Sometimes we have to try infants on several different brands of formulas, until we find the right one."

Jake looked down at his daughter lying in her mother's arms. "She looks so pale and she seems lifeless."

"Think about how you'd feel if you had just emptied your stomach through vomiting and diarrhea, Mr. Bishop," Dr. Nelson said. "Louisa's weak and not feeling very well right now, but all she needs is breast milk and a lot of TLC from her mommy and daddy. I'd say by tomorrow, she'll be her happy, energetic self again."

Jake let out a deep breath that he hadn't even been aware he'd been holding. He suddenly realized just how frightened he'd been. Damn, what a bitch to care about somebody so much that the thought of losing them could drive you crazy! And he wasn't the only one who had suffered the fear of the damned. Donna's body trembled against his.

"It's all right, sugar," he said. "Louisa's going to be just fine. And we're going to give her all that tender loving care the doctor prescribed."

As Jake led Donna out of the examining room, Dr. Nelson followed them into the hall. "If you need me for anything, just call the office or my answering service."

"Thanks, Doc," Jake said.

"Yes, thank you." Donna held her baby close to her body.

Sheila and Caleb were in the waiting area when Donna and Jake emerged. They rushed toward them.

"She's fine," Jake said. "The baby-sitter gave Louisa some formula that didn't agree with her."

Lindsay Crabtree cringed as she came forward and reached out to caress Louisa's cheek. "I'm so sorry. I had no idea Louisa shouldn't have the formula. She'd finished off the two bottles of breast milk Mrs. Bishop left and she still seemed hungry. I—I thought I was doing the right thing."

"It wasn't your fault," Donna assured her. "It was my

fault for not leaving more breast milk and for going out for lunch with Sheila when I should have come home immediately.''

"It wasn't anybody's fault," Jake said. "What happened would have happened whenever we tried Louisa on that formula for the first time. According to Dr. Nelson, she's going to be just fine. So, Lindsay, you go on home and when we need a baby-sitter again, we'll give you a call."

"Gee, thanks, Mr. Bishop." Lindsay's lips curved into a frail smile. "I wouldn't let anything bad happen to Louisa. Not for the world."

"We know that," Donna said.

"Come on. Let me get my two girls home." Jake escorted them out to his Jeep, secured Louisa's carrier into place in the car seat, then strapped Donna's safety belt before he got in up front, on the driver's side. He stuck his head out the window. "Hey, Sheila, get somebody down at the garage to bring Donna's car home sometime later today."

Sheila nodded and waved. Jake glanced into the back seat at his wife. Tears trickled down her face.

"It's all right," he said. "Louisa is going to be fine."

Donna reached over into the front seat, grabbed Jake's shoulder and squeezed. "I'm so glad we have you. All I could think about was that I wanted you and needed you. Then I looked up…and there you were."

# Seven

Jake stood in the middle of the bedroom, his arms crossed over his chest, his gaze fixed on the sleeping woman. Never before had he felt so much like a man—a man in charge of his world, taking care of what belonged to him. All his life he had avoided responsibilities and commitments, always uncertain whether or not he was capable of making a relationship work. He'd never thought of himself as husband and father material. But today's events had proven something to him, something vitally important to his future. Not only had he *been there* for his wife and child, he had actually taken charge of the situation.

He'd been scared—more frightened that he'd ever admit to anyone. In a few short weeks his daughter had become the center of his universe. He'd never thought it possible to love someone so much. And he knew Donna loved their child in the same way.

Jake lifted the quilt folded at the foot of the bed and

spread it over Donna's sleeping form. She'd been emotionally exhausted by the time they arrived home an hour ago. He had insisted she rest and let him look after Louisa. She hadn't resisted the suggestion, indeed, she had readily agreed.

He couldn't forget the gratitude in her eyes or the way she'd said, *I'm so glad we have you. All I could think about was that I wanted you and needed you.* He chose to believe that those words had come straight from her heart and that she wouldn't take them back later.

Jake liked the idea of her needing him, wanting him. Of her being glad he was a part of Louisa's life—a part of her life. If anyone had told him six months ago that not only would he soon be a husband and father, but that he actually would have demanded those roles, he wouldn't have believed them.

Jake enjoyed watching Donna—awake or asleep. She possessed a fiery beauty that aroused him on numerous levels. He would like nothing better than to lie beside her, waken her with kisses and undress her slowly. Just the thought of taking her with the same hot passion they'd known last summer hardened his body painfully. She was his wife and yet she wasn't. *In name only.* His mind might accept that stipulation, but his body didn't.

Turning abruptly so that he didn't have to look at the woman he so desperately wanted, Jake gazed down into the basinet. Louisa stared up at him with dark brown eyes identical to his. He could never put into words the feelings inside him whenever he looked at his sweet baby girl. This child had changed his life irrevocably, giving it meaning and purpose. Maybe he'd never done anything right ever before, but he was going to get fatherhood right—no matter what it took.

''Hello, Sugar Baby,'' Jake whispered as he leaned over

and lifted his little girl into his arms. "Let's you and me get out of here and let Mommy sleep. She's had a rough day. Your getting sick took a lot out of her. You'll find out that a mother gets awfully upset when anything happens to her baby."

Jake carried Louisa out into the hall and down the stairs. "Of course, daddies get upset, too, but since we're big, strong men, we have to pretend that we're not upset, that we've got it all together."

Louisa cooed and once again Jake could have sworn she smiled at him. "I'll bet you need a diaper change, don't you? I can handle that, but if you get hungry, we'll have to wake up your mama."

After entering the den, Jake laid Louisa down on the sofa, then reached over and pulled a diaper from the pastel polka dot diaper bag Donna had left lying on the cushions. He unsnapped his daughter's pink sleeper, but before he could remove her wet diaper, the phone rang. He cursed under his breath. Hurriedly, he slipped the clean diaper into place and secured the tabs, then lifted Louisa onto his shoulder and made it over to the phone by the fourth ring.

"Yeah!"

"Hello to you, too," Caleb said.

"Sorry," Jake chuckled. "I was in the middle of changing Sugar Baby's diaper and I was afraid the phone would wake Donna."

"So, how's everything going?"

"Fine."

"Have you got everything under control?" Caleb asked.

"I think so. Donna's resting and I'm taking care of my daughter."

"No more vomiting or diarrhea?"

"Nope. She seems right as rain."

"Sheila wanted me to make sure you didn't need us to come over tonight and help out."

"Thanks for offering, but we should be all right."

"Jake?"

"Yeah?"

"You're a good father." Caleb cleared his throat. "If you ever start doubting yourself, stop and remember that you aren't our old man any more than Hank is or I am. There is no Bishop curse when it comes to fatherhood."

"I'll try to remember that."

"If you need us, give us a call."

"Yeah, thanks."

Jake sat in the rocker by the fireplace, laid Louisa in his lap and snapped her sleeper together. She wriggled and cooed. And Jake's heart swelled with love and pride.

"Caleb's right. I'm not my old man." He leaned over, brought Louisa's little fist to his lips and kissed her hand. "No matter how scared I am that I'll mess up, I'm going to do my darnedest to be a good father. I promise that I'll be around all the time and I'll take care of you—and your mother, too, if she'll let me."

Donna stood in the doorway; her breath caught in her throat as she listened to Jake's vows to their daughter. She was drawn to him in a way she'd never been to any other man—not even Edward. There was something so strong and capable about Jake, and yet so tender and kind. The man she had shared a weekend with last summer had been passionate and demanding and exciting—a lover she could never forget. But she hadn't guessed that inside J.B. there existed a loving, caring man, capable of being a good father to her child. She had neither expected nor wanted Jake Bishop to be a part of their lives, but circumstances had left her little choice but to marry him and accept him as Louisa's father.

Watching him with their child always stirred deep feelings within Donna, feelings she wanted no part of—now or ever. She could not—would not—allow herself to love Jake. But how could she stop herself from wanting him?

"Who was that on the phone?" she asked as she entered the den.

Jake jerked his head up and stared at Donna, his eyes wide with surprise. "Sorry, if it woke you. That was Caleb, checking on us."

"Did you tell him that you had everything under control? Wife tucked away in bed after her mini nervous breakdown and daughter safe in your arms."

"Yeah, I told him something like that." Jake caressed Louisa's back. "Feeling better after your nap?"

"Yes, thanks. I'm not nearly as shaky as I was." Donna sat on the sofa. "I've never been so frightened in my life. I had no idea what was wrong with Louisa."

"We can be grateful that it was something simple and that she recovered so quickly." Holding Louisa up to his face, Jake nuzzled her cheeks. "No more formula for you, huh, Sugar Baby? Just mother's milk from now on."

"Poor Lindsay. She was devastated." Donna glanced at Jake, her gaze resting on his parted lips. "You were so kind to her. Thank you for reassuring her that we didn't blame her."

"She was beating herself up over something that really wasn't her fault," Jake said.

"Jake— I…about what I said to you today…"

"What did you say to me?" He rocked Louisa, who lay perfectly content in his arms.

"About being glad that we had you and that I wanted you and needed you. I think I should explain what I meant."

"I assumed you meant exactly what you said, that you're

glad Louisa has a father you can count on when you need him.''

Donna breathed a sigh of relief. ''Yes, that's exactly what I meant. I know that, sometimes, my actions have been unforgivable. I even went so far as to tell you that you weren't the type of man I wanted for Louisa's father.''

''Who could blame you?'' Jake shrugged. ''After all, I'm not much of a prize, am I?''

''No, that's not true. You *are* a prize.'' Donna averted her gaze from Jake's face. ''The fact is, you are Louisa's father and you've done everything possible to prove to me that you can be a good father to her. I needed you today. I needed someone who loves Louisa just as much as I do, to share the trauma—the fear of losing her.''

''No matter what happens between you and me, I'll always be around to help with my daughter. I don't ever want her wishing that I wasn't her old man.''

''She's going to love you so much.'' Donna cleared her throat. ''She already knows you and loves you.''

''You don't mind that Sugar Baby and I have bonded?'' Jake kissed his daughter's forehead, then held her against his chest.

''Jake, I...well...''

Rooting around on Jake's chest, Louisa whimpered. Jake stood, walked over and handed his daughter to her mother. ''I think father-daughter bonding time is over. Looks like only you have what she wants now.''

Donna accepted the hungry child as Jake sat beside her on the sofa. She unbuttoned her blouse, lowered the flap on her nursing bra and lifted Louisa to her breast. The child latched on and began nursing greedily.

''She's got the Bishop appetite,'' he said jokingly as he leaned back into the sofa cushions and relaxed.

Donna caressed Louisa's head. Her heart nearly burst

with love. "I have a pretty good appetite myself and if I don't learn to curb it, I'll never lose the extra weight I gained when I was carrying Louisa."

"On you the extra weight looks good." Jake ran his gaze from the top of her head to the tips of her bare feet. "Besides, I like a woman who has an appetite, for food and...for other things."

"Thanks," Donna mumbled, but she couldn't hear the sound of her own voice because her heartbeat drummed so loudly in her ears. Those "other things" Jake had referred to were sexual appetites that she preferred to forget. Appetites that had drawn her into a brief affair based solely on wanton desires.

"I think I'll go on up and take a shower," Jake said. "It's been a long day and I'm about ready to hit the sack."

"Yes, you go on up." Donna kept her gaze focused on the child in her arms. "If you're asleep when I come upstairs, I'll try to be quiet and not waken you."

"If I'm asleep, you could blow up the room and I probably wouldn't wake up. Haven't you noticed what a sound sleeper I am?"

"Yes, of course." She had noticed everything about her husband. And that was a major problem. She'd known it would be difficult to live with Jake, to share a bed with him and be able to resist his magnetic masculine appeal. He was, by any woman's standards, an irresistible man.

"But if you need me during the night, all you have to do is touch me and I'll wake up like that." Grinning devilishly, Jake snapped his fingers, then turned and walked out of the room.

Touching Jake Bishop was always on her mind. Fear that she might touch him in her sleep and invite his attentions. Yet at the same time she felt a great longing to touch him, run her hands over his hard body. Touching Jake would be such sweet agony. And a mistake for which she would pay dearly.

*Haven't you learned your lesson?,* asked that pesky inner voice. *You and Jake are a lethal combination. One touch creates sparks that set you both on fire.*

Jake took his time in the bathroom, all the while wondering just how long it would be before Donna came upstairs. Unless his instincts were way off, his wife had sex on her mind. He knew women and he knew Donna. She hadn't been with a man since their weekend in New Mexico last summer. She had to be needing it bad by now. But would she come to him and admit that she wanted him? Or would she go on fighting her needs and denying them both the release only a shared night of passion could give them?

Tonight could determine the fate of their marriage. He had to say and do all the right things. Maybe Donna needed persuading. Maybe she wanted him to take the initiative. But if he pushed her too far, too fast, he could ruin everything. He could destroy any chance they had to truly become husband and wife.

He showered, shaved and dried his hair, then straightened up the bathroom. Donna liked things neat and tidy, but by nature, he was a slob. He'd lived on his own far too long. Trying to please a woman wasn't easy for him, but if that's what it took to bring Donna back into his arms, he was willing to do it.

Jake pulled on a pair of black briefs, opened the bathroom door and scanned the bedroom. No Donna.

*She's going to stay downstairs until she thinks I'm asleep,* he told himself. *She knows that if I'm still awake, things could get hot and heavy tonight.*

Jake stretched out on the bed and waited. Within ten minutes he grew restless. He wasn't sleepy—he was horny.

But he could hardly rush downstairs and demand that Donna come to bed right this minute. Macho tactics like that didn't work very well on his wife.

Hey, those tactics had worked quite well on the woman he'd met at the Blue Bonnet Grill last summer. She hadn't put up much of a fight once he'd taken her into his arms on the dance floor. Hell! Maybe he was using the wrong strategy. Maybe he'd been too nice, too obliging. Maybe he should revert to type and show Donna just what she was missing when she repeatedly rejected him.

Jake jumped up and turned off all the lights, except the night-light that cast a soft, dim glow over the bedroom. He lay back down, rested his arms behind his head and plotted Donna's imminent downfall. By imagining the way she would look, how she would react, what she would say, Jake prepared himself for the inevitable. Donna would place Louisa in her basinet, then she'd go into the bathroom, bathe, put on her gown and come to bed. He would reach out and touch her. She'd turn to him. And that was all it would take. She'd be his for the rest of the night.

Donna held Louisa, who had been asleep for over thirty minutes. She delayed going upstairs. Waiting, hoping, that Jake would be asleep when she put Louisa in her basinet. With each passing night, it became more and more difficult to sleep beside Jake and not turn to him for physical comfort and release.

*So, would it be so bad if you did have sex with him?* That pesky voice encouraged her to succumb to her desires. *Just because you have sex with him doesn't mean you're going to fall in love with him. And it certainly doesn't mean you have to stay married to him!*

But Donna knew that if she and Jake made love, he might assume she'd changed her mind about their marriage being temporary. Perhaps she could simply tell him—up front—that sex wouldn't change the ground rules. Come December, they were getting a divorce. They had agreed on six months and she expected him to abide by their agreement. But they had also agreed to a marriage in name only—no sex!

Donna rose from the recliner, climbed the stairs and tiptoed down the hallway. After opening the bedroom door, she paused, surveyed the semidark room and sighed with relief when she saw Jake's still form in the bed. He was asleep. Thank goodness.

She crept over to the basinet, quietly eased Louisa into place and then rushed into the bathroom. Breathless, her heart beating wildly, Donna leaned back against the closed door and shut her eyes. *Please, please,* She silently pleaded, *let Jake continue sleeping. If I can make it through tonight without giving in to him, I should be able to resist him for the next few months.*

After drawing a bubble bath, Donna stepped in and soaked for nearly an hour. Every time she ran the washcloth over her body, she shivered. Memories of Jake's caressing hands and attentive lips flashed through her mind.

Stop this! she told herself as she emerged from the tub and wrapped herself in a large, fluffy towel. Think about something besides Jake's expertise as a lover. Remember the kind of man he is. An ex-mercenary. A tough cowboy with nothing to show for his life except the hopes of owning a quarter horse ranch.

He isn't anything like Edward.

That's it! Think about Edward. How much you loved him. How happy the two of you were together.

But Edward was a fading memory. A sweet memory, but no more than that. Jake was a living, breathing man, who was out there in her bedroom, lying in her bed. All she had to do was touch him, whisper his name and he would take her. And take her. And take her!

Donna trembled as her body recalled the unparalleled pleasure of Jake's lovemaking. With shaky fingers, she grabbed her gown, slid it over her head and then reached for the doorknob.

*Just go get into bed and go to sleep. Stay on your side. Don't touch him. And if he touches you, do not react.*

Easing back the covers, she hesitated, waiting to see if Jake moved or spoke. He didn't. She crawled into bed and pulled the sheet and blanket up over her shoulders. Tension tightened every muscle in her body. She listened and heard only the sound of Jake's breathing. He is asleep, she told herself. He's asleep and I'm safe for one more night.

She lay there, her back to him. Waiting for her body to relax. Waiting for her mind to shut down. Waiting for sleep. Minutes ticked by—endless minutes of which she lost count. Neither relaxation nor sleep came to her. Only unwanted thoughts of Jake. His dark, piercing eyes. His broad, hairy chest. His big, muscular arms. His deep, throaty laughter.

She smelled the uniquely masculine scent of the man lying next to her. The light citrus aroma of Jake's soap clung to his skin and body hair. She had an almost irresistible urge to bury her face against his chest and breath in the odor of clean manliness.

"What's the matter, sugar, can't you sleep?"

Donna jumped as if she'd been shot. Oh, God, he's not asleep!

"No, I—I supposed I'm too emotionally exhausted to rest," she told him.

He rolled over so that his body touched hers. She sucked in a deep breath. Lowering his head so that his lips were against her ear, he nuzzled her neck.

"What you need is a massage."

*No, please, don't let him touch me.*

His big hand clamped down on her shoulder. She trembled from head to toe. As he sat up and braced his back against the headboard, he pulled Donna into a sitting position between his legs.

"Relax, sugar." He grasped her shoulders. "You're way too tense."

The moment he caressed her through the thin cotton material of her gown, she moaned quietly. A tingling sensation came to life in her femininity and within seconds spread outward through her whole body. She loved the feel of his big hands as they kneaded her shoulders.

"You don't play fair," she said. "Please, Jake, I don't want this. I don't—"

"Yes, you do." He leaned down and kissed her neck. "Why are you fighting it, sugar? Why don't you just let it happen? Remember how good it is between you and me?"

Yes, she remembered. Every touch. Every kiss. Every wild and passionate moment.

"But it's just sex," she said breathlessly. "We don't love each other and we aren't going to stay married."

"Is that what's bothering you?" Jake nipped her ear as he slid his hands down her arms and across to cup her breasts in his palms. "If it is, then stop worrying. I'm not asking for anything more than tonight and the pleasure we can give each other."

His thumbs raked across her nipples. Coming to life, her breasts pressed against the confining material of her gown. She moaned as ripples of longing undulated through her body.

She should tell him that this wasn't what she wanted, that their making love would only complicate an already terribly complicated situation. But why should she lie to herself and to him? Why should she deny them both the chance to release some of the nerve-racking tension that radiated between them? Hadn't he just said that he didn't expect more than this one night? Wasn't that concern the reason she was so uncertain, so afraid?

She turned in his arms. Their gazes met and held. He clasped her face in his big hands, brought his mouth down on hers and kissed her with gentle force. Her body throbbed with need. She opened her mouth and invited his invasion. He plunged and plundered, deepening the kiss, as he cupped the back of her head with one hand. Lowering his other hand between them, he unbuttoned her gown, slipped his hand inside and covered her breast. Lightning flashes of sensation zigzagged from her breasts to her femininity.

When they were both out of breath, Jake eased his mouth from hers and painted a moist trail down her throat. She tossed back her head, allowing him full access. His tongue delved inside the front of her gown, seeking out the lush sweetness of her breast. When he licked her, she cried out as intense pleasure burst inside her.

"Oh, Jake. Jake." She moaned his name several times as she threaded her fingers through his hair, encouraging his tender assault on her breasts.

When he lifted her enough to catch the hem of her gown, she cooperated fully and allowed him to remove the thin cotton garment. She sat there on the bed, completely naked, her skin sensitive to his touch, her nipples beaded, her feminine core clenching and releasing as moisture gathered between her thighs.

"I know what you need, sugar. Please, let me love you." Jake skimmed her body with his fingertips, lingering over her breasts. Then he explored the secrets of her moist folds.

She squirmed against his hand as she sought relief. While

he petted her, she reached out and tugged on his briefs. He lifted his hips to assist her in removing his only garment.

She could make out the silhouette of his big body in the semi-darkness, but she needed more than that shadowed glimpse. So much more. She circled his erection. His deep, husky groan pleased her.

"I need you so, Jake. Please, make love to me." She could no longer fight both her own wanton desires and his overwhelming masculinity.

With her permission, he devoured her, nibbling, licking, sucking, until she writhed on the bed in an agony of sensuality. He parted her thighs. She shivered when his tongue slid up her inner thigh. She held her breath as his mouth moved higher and higher, finally stopping when he reached his destination. The moment his lips made intimate contact with her damp flesh, Donna cried out. Jake lifted her hips, bringing her closer to his marauding mouth. Then he began a slow, sensual attack that soon had her weeping as her body coiled tighter and tighter. With one final sweep of his tongue, he snapped the cord and flung her into a release so intense that uncontrollable shudders racked her body.

Before she had a chance to recover from the intense climax, Jake rose up and over her. She reached out for him, wanting him inside her, needing all of him. He cupped her hips, lifted them to meet his thrust and plunged deeply and completely. They twisted and turned on the bed, exchanging positions of dominance, while their bodies joined in a passionate frenzy.

When her body tightened, Jake knew she was on the verge of another climax. He accelerated the pace, taking her harder and faster. The moment she spun out of control, his release hit him full-force. The power of their simultaneous completion shattered them into a million shards of pleasure.

As the aftershocks rippled through their bodies, they lay in each other's arms, their bodies wet with perspiration, their breaths ragged and their lips seeking contact. They kissed with tenderness, each needing the continued loving. He caressed her hip. She curled his chest hair around her fingers.

She felt as wanton and wicked as she had last summer, when she'd spent the weekend in a sexual haze. How was it possible that being in Jake's arms turned her into a hussy capable of anything?

When she tried to pull away from him, he wrapped his arms around her, dragged her on top of him and whispered, "Ah, sugar, don't run off so soon. The night's just begun."

She closed her eyes and listened to the loud, steady beat of his heart. All she wanted to do was drape her body around his and stay right where she was forever.

"Louisa will wake soon. She'll need to be changed and fed," Donna said, lying on Jake, her whole body attuned to his.

"And when she does, you'll take care of her." Jake rubbed Donna's damp back, then lowered his hands to stroke her buttocks. "Afterward, when Louisa is asleep again, how about letting me take care of you?"

"Jake…I—"

"Don't say no, not when you want it as much as I do." He nuzzled the side of her face until she turned enough so that he could capture her mouth. When he ended the ardent kiss, he mumbled against her moist lips, "Just for tonight."

Jake awoke at dawn and realized Donna wasn't in the bed with him. Lifting himself up on one elbow, he leaned over and looked down into the basinet. Louisa slept like an angel. So, where was Donna? He scanned the room quickly and discovered the French doors leading onto the balcony were open. He flung back the covers, got up and strolled out onto the balcony. Donna stood there in the moonlight, the warm summer breeze swaying the nearby tree branches, which created wavy shadows across her body. A body he knew as well as he knew his own. After she had nursed Louisa and returned their child to her basinet, he had explored his wife's lush body with delight and appreciation. Their second mating had been more leisurely than the first, with the added pleasure of extensive foreplay.

"Donna?"

She jumped and gasped simultaneously, then glanced over her shoulder. "I'm all right. Go back to bed, Jake. I just need some time alone to think things through." She turned her attention to the night sky.

"Sometimes, you do too much thinking." He slipped his arms around her and tugged her back against his chest. "I like you better when you're feeling and not thinking."

"You know that we can't base a marriage—a life together—on sex, no matter how good it is."

"And it is good, isn't it?" Lowering his head alongside hers, he rubbed his rough chin against her smooth cheek.

"We have an agreement and nothing has changed because of…what happened."

"We're still getting a divorce come December, right? Is there some reason you thought you needed to remind me of that fact?"

"I didn't want you to think that our making love had changed anything between us," she said.

"Are you sure I'm the one you're trying to convince?"

She whirled around in his arms and glared at him. "What do you mean by that?"

Jake eased his index fingers up the outer side of Donna's bare arms. She shivered. "Maybe you're afraid that what happened between us tonight changed things for you. Is that what's bothering you?''

''No, of course not.''

''Then we don't have a problem, do we?'' He turned and walked into the bedroom, knowing that what they'd shared tonight *had* changed things for both of them. But he was willing to admit the truth, only if Donna was able to admit it, too. He figured it would take more than one night to bring her around to his way of thinking. He just had to bide his time, take advantage of every opportunity and make love to his wife as often as she'd allow. After all, he had until December to persuade Donna that they should stay married.

# Eight

The grandfather clock in the foyer chimed four times. Donna fidgeted in the armchair, her gaze checking the doorway. Jake came in from the ranch at various times—anywhere from five to seven, depending upon his workload for the day. If she were lucky, he wouldn't arrive until long after her study club had dispersed. The last thing she wanted was for her social acquaintances to meet Jake while he was hot, sweaty and dirty. Although she thought he was the sexiest man alive no matter what state he was in, she wanted to shield him from her colleagues' judgmental glances. And protect herself from more gossip.

He usually came in through the side door and took a shower in the bathroom adjacent to the den. If he followed his normal routine, she'd hear him when he came in and might have time to usher her friends out the front door before he poked his head in to say hello. What she didn't want was Stephanie Lamont meeting him at all. The woman was sure to give a full report to her uncle, President Harding, on Donna Fields's home life. Tongues were already wagging and speculations on her actions ranged from "She must be insane to have *remarried* that cowboy" to "The man is quite attractive and he *is* Governor Rand's brother-in-law."

Donna glanced into the dining room and saw the woman who had cleaned her home, twice a week, for the past four years. The plump, forty-year-old mother of three also helped out whenever the study club met at Donna's house or whenever she hosted a party. Jimmie Lou Long placed the silver coffeepot on the silver tray atop the buffet, then stared directly at Donna. She nodded her head toward the kitchen. Donna wondered what Jimmie Lou was trying to tell her. Some minor disaster in the kitchen? Whatever it was, she probably needed to check on the matter.

"You do know that Selina Forbes is getting a half-a-million-dollar settlement," Gloria Kirkland said. "She always was a smart girl."

Teetering laughter tinkled throughout the living room. Donna smiled and laughed on cue, but when she glanced back into the dining room, she noticed that Jimmie Lou was still standing there, rolling her eyes and nodding her head repeatedly toward the kitchen. Donna hoped the garbage disposal hadn't gone on the fritz again.

"Now, that's what you should have done, Donna." Patricia Weston reached over and laid her hand on Donna's arm.

Donna turned her attention from Jimmie Lou's peculiar behavior to Patricia's comment. "I beg your pardon?"

"If you had to succumb to a whirlwind romance and get yourself pregnant, you should have found yourself some millionaire instead of a worthless cowboy," Patricia said.

"Lord, yes!" Gloria sighed dramatically. "That way,

when the marriage ended in divorce, you'd wind up with something substantial to show for giving the beast the best years of your life."

Silly laughter rose from the group of five socially prominent ladies. Heat flushed Donna's cheeks. She had known that her so-called friends looked down on Jake, despite the fact that he was the First Lady of Tennessee's brother, but no one had been insensitive enough to malign him in front of her—not until today. But then, this was the first social gathering she'd attended since Louisa's birth and her marriage to Jake.

Donna opened her mouth to tell them that Jake might be penniless, but he wasn't worthless. He was gentle, kind and loving. After their passionate night together three weeks ago, they had made love every chance they got. She realized that by giving in to her very human needs, she ran the risk of caring too much for her husband. Had she fooled herself into believing she wouldn't fall in love with Jake, that she could end their marriage with no regrets?

"I hear your husband is a real hunk," Marcia Duggar said. "Big and dark and even better looking than Caleb Bishop, in an older, more rugged way."

"Jake is—" Donna said.

"Gorgeous or not, did you have to marry him?" Claudia Ryan asked. "He's probably fabulous in the sack, but—"

"Of course she had to marry him." Stephanie set her china cup and saucer down on the end table beside the sofa, then smiled coyly. "Donna is hardly the type of woman who'd have sex with a man and have his child if she weren't married."

Donna realized that everyone sitting cozily together in her living room knew the truth—that she and Jake hadn't married and divorced in a whirlwind romance last summer.

"You certainly aren't going to stay married," Gloria

said. "I mean, what on earth could you and a man like that have in common?"

"I understand that he didn't even graduate from high school," Patricia informed the group. "Amanda Waters told me that Jake Bishop had a reputation as a wild man, a real bad boy, before he left Crooked Oak, when he was eighteen. Seems he not only got involved with his employer's wife, but he stole money from the man."

Donna opened her mouth to speak, but before she could say a word, Gloria piped in, "What on earth were you thinking, getting involved with a man like that? Your mother would be appalled that you'd married so beneath you."

"I hear your uncle hasn't even acknowledged the marriage," Stephanie said.

"Uncle Duncan lives in Europe since he retired and—" Donna said.

"My poor Donna." Marcia shook her head sadly. "Naturally, we all understand that once this man showed up and announced he was Louisa's father, you really had no choice but to marry him."

"You've been married for a couple of months now, surely you can begin divorce proceedings soon." Claudia picked up a cucumber sandwich from her plate.

"I can only imagine what it must be like having to live with such a…a caveman. He's good for sex, but not much else, I suspect." Gloria sipped her coffee. "He's an uneducated, worthless cowboy. I'd make sure his visitation rights with Louisa were very limited. You certainly don't want him contaminating her little mind."

Donna was on the verge of screaming, *Get out of my house and never come back! How dare you talk about my husband that way! He's a wonderful father and Louisa adores him. I adore him.*

"Howdy, ladies." Jake Bishop swaggered into the living room.

The five women looked up and gasped in unison. Donna closed her eyes and uttered a silent prayer for God's help.

A day's growth of dark stubble covered Jake's lean, rugged face. Dust and grime clung to his torn chambray shirt and faded jeans. Damp perspiration spots covered his shirt and sweat trickled down his neck. His moist black hair clung to his head. And he definitely smelled like a man who'd spent the day around horses.

What was he doing home so early and why had he come into the living room in his work clothes?

Oh, God! That was what Jimmie Lou had been trying to tell her—that Jake was in the kitchen. Had he heard everything her hateful friends had said about him? Donna's shoulders slumped. She glanced down at her feet. Sheer feminine instinct told her that this was going to get ugly! Jake wasn't the type of man who would take insults lightly.

Jake walked directly toward Donna, reached down and lifted her out of her chair. Shocked by his actions, she didn't respond in time to stop him from giving her a tongue-thrusting kiss. Despite the fact that her friends were watching, Donna couldn't stop herself from responding. But just as soon as she did, Jake ended the kiss and slid his arm around her waist.

"Introduce me to these good-looking broads. I could hear you gals cackling all the way out in the kitchen."

Forcing a smile, Donna made the introductions. The five guests couldn't seem to keep their eyes off the big, dirty, sweaty man standing in the middle of Donna's antique-filled living room. He looks as out of place as a bull in a china shop, Donna thought.

"Hey, babe, how about getting me a beer?" Jake swatted her backside before he slumped down on the Duncan

Phyfe sofa, right between Gloria and Patricia. Both women gasped and scooted to the edges of the cream-colored cushions, as if they were ready to take flight. Jake flung his arms across the back of the sofa behind each woman.

"Hurry up, honey bunch," Jake told his wife. "Get your butt in gear and go get me a beer. I'm dying of thirst!"

Jake lifted his feet and plopped his dirty work boots down on the antique mahogany coffee table. Five women cried out as if in pain. Jake grinned. Donna closed her eyes and prayed once again for divine intervention. Her husband knew exactly what he was doing—embarrassing her on purpose.

Donna hurried toward the dining room, but didn't make it into the kitchen before Jimmie Lou emerged with an open beer bottle in her hand.

"I tried to tell you that he was in the kitchen," Jimmie Lou whispered. "But you ignored me."

"How long was he out there?" Donna asked

"Long enough to hear every word that was said about him."

Donna grabbed the beer and rushed back into the living room. "Here you are." She handed him the beer.

Jake grabbed the beer, lifted it to his lips and downed half before he set the moist bottle directly onto the shiny wood surface of the coffee table. The women's gazes moved from Jake's grinning face to the offensive bottle marring the perfection of the table's finish.

The minute her friends left, Jake Bishop was a dead man. Donna glared at her husband, who ignored her menacing look.

Jake reached down on the coffee table and picked up the uneaten portion of Gloria's cucumber sandwich, popped it into his mouth, smacked loudly and licked his lips.

Stephanie rose from her chair. "I really think we should be going."

A simultaneous gasp from the five female guests echoed in Donna's ears like the aftershocks of a cannon blast. She wasn't going to kill Jake instantly. Oh, no. She was going to torture him slowly!

One by one, the ladies rose from their seats and made excuses for having to leave. Jake stood, followed the guests toward the foyer and when they paused to say farewell, reached out and swatted Stephanie and Marcia on their backsides.

"You gals stop by anytime." He winked and grinned wickedly.

The women scurried out the front door like rats escaping a sinking ship. The moment Donna closed the front door, she turned, placed her hands on her hips and glowered at Jake.

"What the hell did you think you were doing?" She lifted her hand and pointed her right index finger into Jake's face. "Those women are going to tell everyone I know that my husband is the most uncouth, unmannerly, uncivilized redneck they've ever met! And Stephanie Lamont just happens to be President Harding's niece."

"I don't see what you're so worried about." Jake's cocky grin vanished. "Those women already thought the worst of me. I just made sure that I lived up to their expectations."

"But you aren't uncouth, unmannerly or uncivilized! Why did you have to put on an Academy Award-winning performance?"

"If I'm none of those things, then why didn't you bother to tell your friends that their comments about me were unfounded?" Jake grabbed Donna's shoulders. "Why didn't you defend me?"

"I was going to, but I couldn't get a word in edgewise. Then you came barging in and made a fool of me in front of my study club. I could hardly tell them that you were putting on an act solely for their benefit."

Jimmie Lou cleared her throat. Jake released his tenacious hold on Donna's shoulders and the two of them turned to see the housekeeper, purse in hand, standing behind them.

"I've got everything cleared away and the dishwasher loaded," Jimmie Lou said. "I'll be running along now." She eased past Jake and Donna and made her way quickly out the front door.

Donna stomped her foot. "What must Jimmie Lou think? I wouldn't blame her if she never came back to this house, after the way you behaved this afternoon."

"You worry too damn much about what other people think!" Jake said, then turned and headed up the stairs.

"Take off those filthy boots! You're getting grime all over the floor." Donna glared at Jake's dirty work boots. "And don't you dare walk away from me. I have a few things to say to you."

"You didn't say enough to your friends before they left, and you've already said more than enough to me." Jake sat on the steps, unlaced his boots and tossed them toward his wife. "Here are my filthy boots." He stood, unbuttoned his shirt and flung it onto the floor.

When he unbuckled his belt, Donna huffed disgustedly. "Now, what are you doing?"

"I'm filthy from head to toe, so I thought I'd remove all my offensive attire before I sully your bathroom." Jake undid his belt, unzipped his jeans and stepped out of them.

He stood there, wearing nothing but a pair of white cotton briefs and a stern look on his face. Donna fought the urge to pick up the nearest solid object and throw it at him.

The macho jerk had made a fool of her. Why hadn't he come into the living room, been his charming good-ole-boy self and dispelled all the misconceptions her study club members had about him? Oh, no, he'd had to prove something to her because his feelings were hurt. Or maybe it was more than his feelings. Maybe they had dented his male pride.

But why should she give a damn about his pride when he obviously didn't concern himself with hers?

"There's no excuse for the way you acted!" she told him.

"And there's no excuse for your allowing those women to talk about your husband the way they did."

Jake turned to go up the stairs. Donna gasped when she noticed a huge, dark bruise on his back.

"How did you hurt your back?" she asked.

He paused halfway up the stairs, but didn't turn around. "A horse and I had a little disagreement. That's why I came home early today. So I could take it easy and rest up. And I foolishly hoped my wife would give me a little TLC."

"Did you see a doctor?" Donna took a few tentative steps upward toward her husband. "It looks really bad."

"No need to see a doctor. It'll probably be sore for a couple of days, but it looks worse than it is." Jake continued his climb.

Donna slumped down on the stairs, rested her elbows on her knees and lowered her chin to her folded hands. How had her life come to this? Her nerves were shot. Her mind was a mixed-up jumble. And despite the fact that Jake had embarrassed her shamelessly, a part of her wanted to go upstairs to check on his injured back. The man already had a hold on her, one she knew she had to break free from soon or she'd never be able to escape. Her mind had warned her that becoming lovers with Jake was dangerous, but her traitorous body had succumbed to him time and again.

*He's given you the perfect excuse to end things—now! All you have to do is go upstairs and tell him that you aren't going to have sex with him again, and until your divorce, he has to sleep in another bedroom. You know this is the only way! Do it now, while you're still angry with him.*

Jake flung his briefs onto the tiled floor, turned on the faucets and stepped into the shower. Every muscle in his body ached from having been thrown from that damn unruly stallion. Tension tightened his muscles and jangled his nerves. He couldn't remember the last time he'd been so angry. He'd seen red—literally as well as figuratively—when he'd heard his wife's snobby friends's comments and realized that she wasn't going to defend him.

That damn group of holier-than-thou blue-blooded bitches! How could someone as warmhearted and caring as Donna be friends with a bunch of harpies like that? They judged men by their bank accounts and college degrees. And they thought Donna had made the biggest mistake of her life by marrying him!

What hurt him the most wasn't the unkind things those catty shrews had said, but the fact that Donna hadn't said a word in his defense. Was it possible that despite all her reassurances to the contrary, she actually agreed with her high-society friends?

*A man like that! Uneducated, penniless cowboy! Wild man! Bad boy!* Their shrill voices reverberated inside his head, damning him as the worthless piece of trash his grandfather had once accused him of being.

They had implied that not only was he unsuitable to be

Donna's husband, but that he was unfit to be Louisa's father.

*Limit his visitation rights!*

Jake picked up a bar of soap and briskly lathered his chest and arms, then scrubbed the dirt and grime from his body.

Nobody was going to limit his visitation rights! Sugar Baby was his pride and joy. He adored her and she him. Surely, Donna wouldn't pay any attention to that bunch of snobs. She had promised him six months to bond with his daughter and unlimited visitation rights in the future. If he had his way, the marriage wouldn't end come December and he'd get the chance to be a full-time father to his child.

The very thought of having Sugar Baby cut out of his life soured his stomach. Once he had cleaned up enough to walk on Donna's spotless floors, he was going to have a talk with the lady and get a few things straight.

Maybe he had acted like a macho jerk and embarrassed the hell out of her. So what? Hadn't that been his intention when he'd strutted into the living room? In retrospect, he wasn't sure he'd had any intentions, that he'd actually thought things through at all. He had acted purely on instinct, like a wounded animal striking out at his attackers. When he'd overheard those women talking about him, he'd been so sure Donna would jump to his defense, so sure she would sing his praises. But she hadn't said a word. She'd sat there and let them slander her husband.

Jake lathered and scrubbed and repeated the process twice. God, his back hurt like hell and he was probably going to be sore for several days! He supposed he should have gone to the emergency room and gotten a shot for the pain, but he had—foolishly—thought Donna would take care of him when he came home.

*Bishop, you're an idiot! You're not really her husband.*

*You're just a temporary fixture around here. When are you going to get it through your head that the lady doesn't want you in her life on a permanent basis? She doesn't think you're good enough for her!*

The truth of those words rang in his ears as he stepped out of the shower, dried off and wrapped a towel around his waist.

You're good enough to be a six-month husband to legitimize her daughter and save her job, he told himself. You're even good enough to be her lover. But you'll never be good enough for her to love.

"Jake?" Donna called from the bedroom.

He flung open the bathroom door. Donna stared at him, taking him in from head to toe. Before she could mask her desire, he saw the hunger in her eyes and knew she wanted him. That's the way it always was between them—they might not be in love, but they sure couldn't get enough of each other.

"We need to talk." Donna's gaze raked him from shoulders to knees. "I'll go check on Louisa while you put on some clothes."

"I peeped in the nursery before I took my shower and she was sound asleep."

"Then I'll wait out in the hall."

"Why so formal, sugar? You've seen me naked every night for the past three weeks." He loosened the towel from his waist and dropped it to the floor. "You've been touching and licking and kissing—"

Jerking around quickly, she turned her back on him. "Becoming lovers again was a big mistake. I should have known—"

Jake came up behind her, grabbed her shoulders and lowered his head to whisper in her ear. "You should have known that your friends wouldn't approve of me. You should have known that I could never be worthy of being your real husband, of taking the place of a man like Edward Fields.''

"You could never take Edward's place.''

Jake whirled her around so that she faced him. He released her and said, "Yeah, I know. Edward was a saint. A perfect gentleman, an extraordinary husband, and you'll always love him.''

*No, no!* Donna wanted to scream. *I don't love Edward. I had to learn how to stop loving in order to survive. Edward doesn't stand between us. The pain of losing him is what will prevent me from ever loving another man—even someone as wonderful as you.*

Jake glared at her, his dark eyes black with rage. "Edward isn't flesh and blood, sugar. I am. He can't hold you in his arms and kiss you and make love to you. But I can. And even if you still think you're in love with your dead husband, I know that you want me as much as I want you.''

"No, Jake. Not this time.'' Donna started backing away from him. "Sex isn't going to fix this. It won't change anything.''

He stalked her, his movements panther-like in their slow precision. When he backed her up against the wall, he braced his hands on either side of her head. "No matter what your fancy friends think of me and no matter how you lie to yourself, you're my woman and we both know it!''

He grabbed the back of her head. She gasped. Her eyes widened into large circles when he speared his fingers into her hair. He cupped her hip and tugged her up against his arousal.

"I don't want this," she said, her voice breathless.

"Sure you do." He ground his hardness against her mound and smiled devilishly when she moaned.

"Jake. Please." She tried to move away from him, but he tightened his hold on her hair. She cried out. He slipped his arm around her waist and pressed her breasts against his chest.

"Haven't you punished me enough?" she asked. "You embarrassed me in front of my friends. Wasn't that revenge enough for—"

He ran the tip of his tongue over her lips. She sucked in her breath. He eased his big hand up her thigh, lifting her skirt to her hips and caressing her buttocks. He pulled her face up into his, plunged his tongue into her mouth and devoured her lips. She squirmed and wriggled. Refusing to release her, he held her tightly, fiercely, possessively.

Her mind fought against him, but her body ceased the battle and responded. She slid her arms around him, returned his kiss and made no further protest when he lifted her into his arms and carried her across the room to the bed. He ripped the clothes from her body in a sensual fury, all the while telling her in the crudest terms exactly what he was going to do to her.

When he came down over her, his mouth seeking her breast, she bucked up to meet him and cried out as he entered her with one swift lunge. He set the pace—fast and furious. She quickly picked up the beat. Nothing mattered. Not Jake's sore back. Not Donna's common sense. Not the fact that they didn't love each other. Not the knowledge that sex couldn't solve their problems.

The only thing that mattered was satisfying the raging hunger inside them.

They mated with an untamed fury, giving and taking, loving and being loved. The tension inside them built steadily with each thrust, each bump, each heated word, each biting kiss, until they were both wild with the need for fulfillment. Donna's body tightened. She cried out her pleasure when release rocketed through her body. Jake pumped into her with jackhammer speed. His climax claimed him with an intensity that drained him completely. He fell onto Donna, then tumbled her over and pulled her against his side. She clung to him as the aftershocks of completion echoed through her body.

"Now, tell me that you don't want me," Jake said.

# Nine

Donna lay in Jake's arms, relaxed and content, completely sated from their heated lovemaking. Her mind began to function just enough for her to question her own sanity. What had she done? Instead of ending her physical relationship with Jake, she'd had sex with him again. Now it would be twice as difficult to ask him to move out of her bedroom. Just as she forced herself to move, a boisterous cry came through the baby monitor.

Donna sat straight up in bed. "Louisa!"

Jake gently grasped her shoulders and shoved her down onto the rumpled bedspread. "I'll go get her, sugar. It won't hurt her to cry for a couple of minutes. You just take it easy."

Big, naked and gloriously male, Jake stood, rushed into the bathroom and returned a couple of minutes later wearing a pair of clean briefs. Donna watched his every move. Even now, knowing that she had to garner the strength to

end their relationship, she found him irresistible. She loved
the width of his shoulders, the muscular leanness of his big
body, the thick, curly hair that covered his arms and legs
and created a vee from his chest to his navel. She loved
everything about Jake Bishop. Absolutely everything. And
if she wasn't careful, she'd wake up one morning and find
herself in love with the man.

*You do not love him! You cannot love him. You've loved
and lost once, and once in a lifetime is more than enough.
Remember how you felt when Edward died, when you lost
not only your husband, but your sanity. You promised yourself that if you ever recovered, you would never allow yourself to be hurt like that again.*

Jake's voice came through the monitor on the bedside
table. He was jabbering baby talk to their daughter. Her
big, rugged cowboy had turned out to be a doting father, a
man truly devoted to his child.

"Mama's waiting for you, Sugar Baby," Jake said. "Let
Daddy change your diaper and then Mama will feed you."

Donna jumped out of bed, ran into the bathroom, washed
hurriedly and searched her closet for a robe. Just as she
slipped her arms into the sleeves of a yellow-and-white-
striped silk robe, Jake entered the room, Louisa in his arms.

Quickly Donna tied the sash around her waist and
reached out for her daughter. "Mama's girl had a good long
nap, didn't she? Are you hungry, darling?"

Jake handed Louisa to her mother. "How about you?
Are you hungry? I could rustle us up some supper."

"I—I'm not hungry," Donna said as she sat on the bed.
She opened her robe and brought Louisa to her breast.

"I never get tired of looking at you nursing Louisa."
Jake's gaze lingered on Donna's breast. "As a matter of
fact, I never get tired of looking at you, period."

"Jake, I…well, we need to talk, but now isn't the right time."

"What do we need to talk about?" Jake opened the closet door, searched through his clothes until he found a pair of jeans, then removed them from the wire hanger and stepped into them.

"We need to discuss our relationship." Donna caressed her daughter's silky black hair.

"I don't think we need any words when it comes to *discussing* our relationship." Jake removed a black T-shirt from the chest of drawers, slipped it over his head and stuffed it into his jeans. "We communicate better on a non-verbal level."

Donna sighed, knowing Jake was right. Their bodies spoke a language that transcended verbal communication. "About what happened this afternoon—"

"Do you mean the scene with your friends or what we did afterward?" Jake grinned and winked at her as he slumped down in the wing-back chair by the windows, then put on his socks and boots.

"Both events, I suppose," she said.

"I wish I could say that I'm sorry about acting up in front of your friends, but by my estimation, they deserved what they got."

"And did I deserve it, too, Jake? Did I deserve to be embarrassed in front of the ladies in my study club? Women I've known for years. Women who have always respected me."

Jake stood, buckled his belt and glared at Donna. "I don't know, sugar. Did you deserve it? I think you did. You allowed those society bitches to talk about me as if I were dirt under their feet."

"I didn't allow them to do anything!" When Donna raised her voice, Louisa released her nipple and whimpered.

She soothed her daughter and the child resumed nursing. Lowering her voice, she said, "I told you that I was going to say something to them, but I didn't get a chance before you came storming in."

"Look, if you want me to apologize to that bunch of snobs, then I'll apologize!"

"It's a little late for apologies. Whatever you might say or do now would only make things worse."

"Then maybe we should consider the subject closed." Jake came over, sat beside Donna on the edge of the bed and slipped his arm around her shoulders. "So what else do we need to discuss?"

Donna scooted away from him. He frowned. She couldn't think clearly when he touched her and right now, she very much needed a clear head.

"Before you used your caveman tactics on me and dragged me off to bed, I was going to tell you that I don't think we should have sex anymore. Making love just clouds the issue and creates problems I don't need."

Jake stared at her, his dark eyes filled with an incredulous, questioning glare. Suddenly he burst into laughter. Loud masculine laughter that shook the room.

Louisa lifted her head and looked at her father. Donna wanted to scream at him, to throw something at him, to pound her fists on his chest. How dare he laugh about such a serious matter!

"This isn't funny," she said.

"Yes, it is, sugar. It's the funniest thing you've ever said. And you know damn well you don't mean it."

"Yes, I do."

"No, you don't. I might have used what you call 'caveman tactics' earlier, but I didn't have to drag you off to bed. You were more than willing. You were eager."

Donna spluttered. "I'm not going to have sex with you

again." She practically hissed the statement through clenched teeth. "I want you to move out of this bedroom tonight!"

Jake's face hardened; his eyes narrowed to slits. "Lady, what's your problem? Why can't you just admit that you enjoy having sex with me—that it's the best part of our marriage."

"That's just it, great sex doesn't make a good marriage."

Jake shot up off the bed. "Well it sure as hell helps!"

"It really doesn't matter, does it? After all, in four months, we're getting a divorce and the only relationship we'll share is being Louisa's parents."

"Why wait four months? Why not get a divorce now?" Jake stomped toward the door, paused for a minute, took a deep breath and said, "Don't wait up for me. I don't know what time I'll be home."

"When you come back, be sure to sleep in one of the other bedrooms," Donna told him.

"Maybe I won't come back. Maybe I'll find a bed somewhere else."

Donna opened her mouth on a silent cry. Maybe he'd find a bed somewhere else? Just what did he mean by that? Did he plan to check into a motel somewhere or did he intend to find himself another woman?

Donna sat on the bed, her body tense, her emotions rioting. So, why should she care if he left her? It didn't matter to her if he spent the night with another woman! Maybe he was right—maybe they should go ahead and get a divorce now. Why prolong the inevitable?

Louisa stirred in her mother's arms. Donna glanced down at the child she so adored. "You're the reason we married, the reason we agreed to remain husband and wife for six months. Your daddy wanted the time to be with you."

Louisa was the one they both loved. Not each other. If

she hadn't gotten pregnant, she and Jake never would have even considered marriage. That long-ago morning when they said goodbye at the airport in New Mexico, neither had thought they'd see the other ever again. And that's the way it should have been.

If only J.B. hadn't turned out to be Jake Bishop. If only Jake hadn't decided, after all these years, to return to Tennessee. Without him in her life, things would be so simple.

In the morning—if Jake came home—she'd tell him that she thought he was right. That they shouldn't wait until December to get a divorce. He could have whatever visitation rights he wanted, if he would just agree to end this farce of a marriage as soon as possible.

The sooner she got Jake out of her bed and out of her house, the better off she'd be.

"Why should I care what Jake's planning to do?" Donna emptied the hamper filled with baby items into the washing machine. "I want that man out of my life."

"You don't mean that and you know it," Sheila said as she handed Donna the box of laundry detergent. "He's your husband and Louisa's father."

Donna measured the right amount of detergent, poured it into the washing machine and adjusted the selection knob. "I never should have married him. Getting involved with Jake Bishop was a mistake from start to finish." She slammed shut the washer lid.

"You don't think Louisa is a mistake and if you hadn't gotten involved with Jake, she wouldn't exist." Sheila laid her hand on Donna's shoulder. "You and Jake are just upset with each other right now, but I'm telling you that if you don't stop him, Jake is going to do something that can end any hopes for your marriage."

"There is no hope for our marriage." Donna walked out

of the laundry room and into the kitchen. When Sheila followed her, Donna turned, looked her friend square in the eye and asked, "What's Jake planning to do? It couldn't be any worse than what he's already done. You wouldn't believe the performance he gave in front of my study club this afternoon."

"That bunch of society snobs!" Sheila laughed sarcastically. "I don't blame him if he put them in their places. Why someone as nice as you would want to be friends with people like Stephanie Lamont and Marcia Duggar is beyond me."

"Stephanie is President Harding's niece and Marcia and I are sorority sisters. And Edward and I were friends with Patricia and Gloria and their husbands."

"And not a one of them showed up at the baby shower Susan and I gave you, did they? That tells me what kind of friends they are."

Donna opened the refrigerator. "Would you like some lemonade? Jimmie Lou made up a fresh pitcher while she was here today."

"Sure, pour us a glass." Sheila sat at the kitchen table. "Too bad Jake won't be drinking lemonade tonight. If he were, he might not be headed for trouble."

Donna let out a long, low, exasperated sigh, lifted the pitcher from the refrigerator and set it on the counter. "So, go ahead and tell me—what is Jake planning on doing tonight? Getting drunk? Well, that doesn't surprise me. I think he's spent a great deal of time in bars."

"When Jake came by the house, he told Caleb that he was going over to the Pale Rider to get rip-roaring drunk."

After taking two tall glasses from the cupboard, Donna poured the lemonade and carried the glasses over to the table. "All I can say is that if Jake does get drunk, he'd better not come back here tonight and make a scene. I'll call the police if he does.'' Donna pulled out a chair and sat beside Sheila.

"According to Jake, he isn't coming home tonight."

"Good."

"Not so good."

"Why? He'll probably come to your house or go over to Hank and Susan's and sleep it off."

"I don't think so." Sheila picked up the lemonade and took a sip.

"Will you stop that! Just tell me what you're dying to say."

"Jake told Caleb that he's going to find himself an obliging woman…one who won't order him out of her bed five minutes after they've made love."

Heavy, heart-pounding silence hung in the room like a painful, breath-robbing mist. Donna gulped in air as she tried to control the sudden rage that consumed her. He was going to find himself another woman! Another woman! Jake—her husband—really was going to take another woman into his arms, kiss her, touch her and make love to her.

Donna's hand trembled so badly that she lost her grip on the glass. It toppled over and lemonade spread quickly across the tabletop. Sheila jumped up, grabbed a dish towel and wiped up the sticky-sweet liquid.

"You have to stop him," Sheila said. "No matter why you and Jake got married, you don't want your marriage to end this way."

"How can I stop him? If he wants another woman—"

Standing behind her, Sheila gripped Donna's shoulders. "He doesn't want another woman. He's upset and very angry. He's got some stupid idea that you're still in love with Edward Fields. He wants to hurt you as much as you've hurt him."

"I'd have to care about him for—"

Sheila squeezed Donna's shoulders. "Save the lies for yourself and Jake. You care about him and we both know it. The last thing you want is your husband spending the night with some floozie he picks up at the Pale Rider. People will find out and then they *will* talk."

"They're already talking, I'm sure, after the way he acted in front of my friends this afternoon. He was rude and vulgar and—"

"Go upstairs, change clothes and get your butt over to the Pale Rider," Sheila said. "I'll stay here with Louisa until you get home, no matter how late."

"I don't want him to do something else to embarrass me."

"Of course you don't, so go stop him."

"He is Louisa's father and he shouldn't be acting so irresponsibly, should he?" Donna's gaze questioned her friend.

"Justify your actions any way you need to, but go to the Pale Rider and get your man." Sheila jerked Donna up out of the chair and turned her toward the door leading into the hallway. "Put on a pair of tight jeans and a bright shirt and some dangling earrings and race your Vette over to that roadhouse and find Jake Bishop before some other woman tries to put her brand on him."

"I'm doing this for Louisa's sake," Donna said.

"Sure you are. Absolutely."

Jake sat at the bar, nursing his glass of whiskey. His third glass. Neat. He barely felt a buzz. It would take a lot more liquor to numb his senses and give him the release he needed. More than one woman had given him the eye since he'd walked into the Pale Rider. But he hadn't singled one out—not yet. He needed to be just a little drunker before he made his move. Drunk enough so that when he did take a woman in his arms, he wouldn't be able to distinguish the features of her face and wouldn't much notice that her hair wasn't a thick mahogany mane.

"Hello, good looking." The long-legged brunette at the end of the bar—the one who'd been trying to gain his attention—came up behind him and laid her hand on his shoulder. "Want some company?"

He glanced over his shoulder. She was tall, slender and attractive in an obvious kind of way. Too much blue eye shadow. Too much blush. Hot pink lips and long, sharp, hot pink claws. Her silky blue blouse was unbuttoned enough to reveal the thrust of a pair of small, high breasts.

"Sure thing, su—honey. Have a seat." Jake patted the empty bar stool next to him. "Hey, bud," he called to the bartender, "give the lady a—what do you want?"

"Vodka and tonic." She sat on the stool and wrapped one long, slender leg around Jake's leg. "My name's Betsy. What's yours?"

"Ja—J.B."

The bartender set her drink down in front of her. Betsy lifted the glass and saluted Jake. "Here's to a good time tonight, J.B."

When she took a hefty swig of her drink, Jake lifted his glass and downed the rest of the whiskey, then motioned for the bartender to bring him a refill.

"How about a dance?" Betsy asked, rubbing her foot up and down Jake's leg.

Jake downed his fourth drink, then slid off the stool, grabbed the woman around the waist and led her onto the dance floor. She curled herself around him intimately and laid her head on his shoulder. He swayed with her to the boisterous country hit tune but his mind was elsewhere. In the past, if he'd been this close to a woman, he'd already have a hard-on by now.

Don't worry, he told himself. A few more drinks and it won't matter who she is.

"I don't live far from here," Betsy said. "And my old man's a trucker. He won't be back for a couple of days."

Her old man? She was married? As a general rule Jake didn't fool around with married women. But what the hell? He was a married man now, wasn't he? Maybe Betsy's husband didn't care who she slept with. He knew his wife sure as hell didn't care what he did or with whom he did it!

"Let's finish our dance and get a couple more drinks before we leave," Jake suggested.

"Sure thing, lover. Whatever you want."

Now, that's what he liked to hear from a woman—*whatever you want.* He was tired of playing games with his temporary wife. Tired of playing second fiddle to her dead husband. A man could take only so much before he had enough.

"I like a woman willing to give a man whatever he wants," Jake said.

"I'm your gal. Just ask around."

"I'll bet you're not the type to let a guy make love to you and then tell him to get lost, are you?"

"What happened, J.B., did you last girlfriend tell you she didn't want you anymore? If she did, she must have been nuts."

The music ended. Betsy turned, gripped Jake's hip and laughed. They took a couple of steps before Jake saw the redhead barreling down on them. Donna was headed straight for him. He blinked several times, thinking he was seeing things. What was Donna doing here? And why did she look mad as hell?

He'd never seen Donna in a pair of jeans. She looked as if she'd been melted and poured into the pair she wore tonight. And that bright yellow blouse she had on clung to her large breasts and hugged her small waist.

His sex hardened painfully. He cursed under his breath. No one else could do to him what she did. One look at Donna and he was crazy with desire.

Jake stopped dead-still on the dance floor and waited for his wife's approach. Betsy glanced questioningly at him, then followed his gaze toward the woman coming straight at them.

"Who's she?" Betsy asked.

"My wife."

"Get your hands off my husband," Donna told the other woman.

"Look, sister, all we was doing was dancing."

"And that's all you're going to do." Donna stuck her finger in Betsy's face. "I said, let go of him."

"Now, look here, just who do you think you are talking to me like that?" Betsy released her hold on Jake, took a step toward Donna and confronted her.

"I told you. I'm his wife."

Betsy grinned as she glanced at Jake. "So, is she the one who isn't willing to give you what you want?"

Jake's muddled brain registered that Donna was angry, that Betsy was taunting her, and that he was in big trouble. "Oh, she gave me what I wanted all right, but afterward, she kicked me out and told me she didn't want me anymore."

Donna's cheeks blazed crimson. "What did you tell this two-bit tramp about us?"

"Two-bit tramp!" Betsy shoved Donna. "You're an idiot. That's what you are, throwing out a man like J.B. Were you crazy?"

Donna shoved Betsy. "My marriage and my husband aren't any of your business, you skinny hussy."

"Well, let me tell you something, if you don't want J.B., I do!" Betsy shoved Donna again, then grabbed Jake's arm and gave Donna a triumphant look.

Temporarily unbalanced by Betsy's hard shove, Donna staggered backwards. She bumped into an empty table near the dance floor. Grasping the table's edge to steady herself, she noticed a mug of beer that had been left untouched. She grabbed the mug and stomped across the dance floor toward her husband and his dance partner. She jerked the woman from Jake's arms, lifted the mug and poured the beer over her head. Betsy spluttered and cursed as the golden brew dripped off her nose and glistened on her flushed face like yellow raindrops.

"Now you've done it, Jake Bishop! You've turned me into somebody I don't know—somebody capable of hunting my husband down at a sleazy honky-tonk and making a public spectacle of myself!"

Donna turned and ran.

"Are you all right?" Jake asked Betsy.

"Yeah, I'm okay." Betsy grinned as she wiped the beer from her face. "You'd better go after her, J.B. I think your wife still wants you."

"Yeah, I think she does."

Jake caught up with Donna in the parking lot. He grabbed her just as she opened the door to her Corvette. He whirled her around to face him.

"Calm down, sugar."

She fought him like a wildcat, flinging her arms, trying to escape his grasp. "I will not calm down! I hate you! Do you hear me? I hate you for making me act like a crazy woman."

"Why did you come after me?" He dragged her toward his Jeep.

"Don't ask me! I have no idea. Chalk it up to temporary insanity."

Jake shoved her up against the Jeep, pressed his body into hers and took her mouth in a wet, hard kiss. She struggled against him at first, but when he deepened the kiss, she responded. The kiss went on and on, until they were both breathless, then Jake eased his mouth from hers and buried his face against the swell of her breasts revealed by the vee of her blouse.

"You were going to have sex with that woman, weren't you! How could you, Jake! How could you!"

"No, sugar, you got it all wrong. What I found out to-night is that you are the only woman I can make love to now." He ground his arousal against her.

She moaned as Jake cupped her buttocks, tugged her up and into him and rubbed his hardness against her mound. Then he crushed his lips into hers. Standing on tiptoe, she flung her arms around him. He swept her off the ground, carried her around to the rear of the Jeep and unlocked the door. Still kissing her, he pushed her inside the back of the Jeep, then dove in beside her.

"What—what do you think you're doing?" she asked as she looked up at him, her eyes filled with undisguised passion as he unsnapped and unzipped her jeans.

Lifting her legs and tugging the jeans down her legs, he replied, "I'm going to make love to my wife."

# Ten

The pole lights cast a mellow yellow-white glow over the roadhouse parking lot. A warm summer breeze rustled through the nearby treetops, but did nothing to alleviate the humidity in the air. Off in the distance, thunder rumbled and shards of heat lightning crackled in the sky. Tim McGraw's distinctive voice drifted outside, coming from one of the CDs the owners of the Pale Rider played during the local band's twenty-minute break. The music mixed and mingled with the other night sounds—a car horn down the highway, the cicadas' buzzing chant, the far-off thunder and the loud beating of two hearts. The lyrics to "One of These Days" told the story of love, rejection, heartache and self-worth.

Donna lay beneath Jake, not assisting him, but not hindering him, either, as he pulled off her shoes and finished removing her jeans. Her femininity tightened, sending an almost unbearable ache through her entire body. "You want to make love here?'' she asked. ''In the back of your Jeep?''

''Yeah, right here and now!'' Rising up and over her, he straddled her hips, then slid her panties down and off.

''Jake, we can't!'' She tried to shove him away, but she couldn't budge his large, muscular body. ''Not here. What if someone sees us?''

''Nobody's going to see us.'' Hurriedly, Jake undid his jeans, then cupped her hips and lifted her up to him. ''Not if we hurry.''

''You're crazy!'' Laughing, she grabbed his shoulders and urged him to take her. She'd never wanted anything more.

''We're both crazy, sugar!'' He thrust, deeply, completely, taking her with the urgency his body demanded.

''Oh, Jake!'' She clung to him, reveling in the feel of him deep inside her. There was no sensation on earth as exquisite as joining her body to his, in becoming one with Jake.

He was right—they were both crazy. But she didn't care. As with every other time she'd been in Jake's arms, nothing mattered except the two of them and the uncontrollable desire that dominated their actions. As if they were two mindless creatures, unable to resist the hot, sizzling passion that ignited between them every time they touched, they made love.

''You're so hot and wet and tight,'' he moaned against her breast, then suckled her through the barrier of her blouse and bra.

She writhed beneath him as his scorching, wet mouth took hers in a kiss that sent off skyrockets inside her head. With each hard, demanding lunge of his body, Jake claimed her, branded her and made her his.

She could feel herself on the verge of unraveling, coming

apart completely. She wanted to make it last, for the incredible sensations to go on and on forever, but she knew the end was near.

"Faster," she murmured, matching him thrust for thrust.

In a voice dark and deep and barely human, barely audible, he made crude, savage utterances that excited her beyond all reason.

Jake's body tightened. He gritted his teeth. Donna dug her nails into his lean hips and cried out, asking him for all he had to give. The moment he accelerated the pounding pace, completion crashed over her like a tidal wave of pleasure. She screamed his name and strummed her throbbing body against his until she drained every ounce of fulfillment from her climax.

Before the last aftershocks rippled through Donna, Jake jetted into her. His climax was so intense that he shuddered and moaned repeatedly as the uncontrollable sensations rippled along his nerve endings.

Collapsing on top of her, he sought her lips with his. Kiss after hungry kiss, they clung to each other. There in the dark confinement of his Jeep, they lay together, listening to their ragged breaths and thumping hearts.

Thunder rumbled closer. Sky-to-ground heat lightning drew nearer. Jake rolled over and off Donna, zipped his jeans and rummaged around, seeking hers. When he found them, he helped her into them, then grabbed her hands and pulled her out of the Jeep.

"Let's go home, sugar," he said.

"Jake, I—"

"No more talking," he told her. "That's when we get in trouble—when we talk." He opened the passenger door.

"But we'll have to talk, sooner or later." She allowed him to help her into the Jeep.

"Let's make it later. Much later." He slammed the door, rounded the hood and got in on the driver's side.

"Jake, please, listen to me," she said when he inserted the key into the ignition.

He paused, turned to her and snorted. "No, you listen to me for a change. I don't care what you say about not wanting me in your bedroom or your bed, or if you think you're still in love with your dead husband. I'm telling you that you're lying to yourself."

"Please…you don't understand—"

"No woman would do what you did tonight unless she cares about a man. Don't you see? You were jealous." Jake started the engine and backed the Jeep out of the parking place.

"I wasn't jealous!" *Liar,* that pesky inner voice chided. *Liar, liar, pants on fire!* Oh, shut up! she told herself.

"The hell you weren't! You *were* very jealous." Chuckling, Jake glanced her way as he drove onto the highway and headed toward home.

"I went to the Pale Rider tonight to keep you from making a big mistake." Donna crossed her arms over her chest. "You would have regretted having sex with that woman."

"You want to know the truth?" Jake blew out a deep, steading breath. "The only way I could have made love to her or any other woman was if I'd pretended she was you."

Jake kept his gaze riveted to the dark road ahead. He'd just made a major confession, something he wasn't accustomed to doing. He'd never been the type for baring his soul to anyone, least of all to a woman. But Donna wasn't just any woman. She was Sugar Baby's mama—and she was his wife. *His wife.* The more he said it, the better he liked it. How was it possible that one fiery redheaded Southern belle had caught him, roped him and branded him with so little effort, when dozens of other women had tried and failed?

Donna sat quietly, uncertain how to respond to Jake's comment. *Don't care about me,* she wanted to tell him. *Because I can't let myself love you. Not ever.*

She cleared her throat. "I came after you tonight to stop you from embarrassing me again. You made such a fool of yourself and of me this afternoon, in front of my study club, that I didn't want Louisa's father to do something even worse." She stole a glance at Jake, who didn't so much as flinch. "I did what I did for Louisa's sake."

"Is that so?" Jake clenched the steering wheel with white-knuckled fierceness. "You made love with me in the back of this Jeep for Louisa's sake?"

"No, that's not what I meant and you know it!"

"Were you hoping we'd make a little brother or sister *for* Louisa?" Jake grinned wickedly.

"Oh, my God! We didn't use any protection!"

"No, we didn't," he said. "So there's no telling what might result from our little tumble. After all, I used a condom every time, last summer, and you still got pregnant with Louisa."

Groaning with self-disgust, Donna covered her face with her hands. "My life has been one long, insane roller-coaster ride ever since you showed up at Susan and Hank's wedding!"

"Are you complaining or telling me that you've enjoyed the ride?" Jake's laughter rumbled like the thunder that seemed to be chasing them.

"How can you laugh about something so serious?"

"You know, sugar, that's one of your problems—you can't laugh about anything lately. You're so uptight about things that you won't allow yourself to enjoy what we have together."

"And just what do we have together?" she asked, her voice sharp, her tone snappish.

"You can ask me that, after what we just shared?" Jake shook his head. "Dammit, woman! Why can't you admit how you really feel about me? Why can't you accept the fact that, despite what your snooty friends think, you and I are good together? And we're good *for* each other. Half the marriages in the world aren't based on anything as strong as what we share."

Jake was right. He knew it. She knew it. But did she dare admit that she agreed with him?

"I figure the longer we stay married, the more likely we are to make a go of it," he said. "I know the idea of marrying an uneducated, penniless cowboy wasn't exactly appealing to you, but I think you should know that I'm not really—"

"It's all right," she said. "It doesn't matter to me that you don't have a formal education or a lot of money. I realized quite some time ago that you're an intelligent man, who has a lot of common sense and has acquired quite a bit of knowledge from the life you've lived. And as far as your being penniless…well, that's something you'll change once you buy the ranch and—"

"I bought the ranch."

"What?"

"That was one of the things I planned to tell you, but we never got around to discussing—"

"Did you get a bank loan?"

"Not exactly."

*Just come right out and tell her. Tell your wife that you paid cash for the quarter horse ranch. Tell her that you're far from penniless.*

"You had to have borrowed the money…oh, the bank

turned you down. Then how— Caleb loaned you the money, didn't he?''

''Donna, I—''

She reached over and caressed his cheek. ''Don't be ashamed that you had to ask your brother for help. You'll pay him back every penny. I know you will.''

''You sure do have a lot of faith in me.'' Jake felt like the lowest of the low for lying to Donna—even if it was lying by omission.

''You're going to make Louisa very proud of you. You'll succeed with the ranch. You'll do it for your daughter.''

''I'd like my daughter…and any other children I might have, to grow up on the ranch. It's an ideal place to raise kids. Fresh air. Wide-open spaces. Trees to climb. Horses to ride. And the house could be renovated.''

''Jake, I probably didn't get pregnant tonight,'' Donna said softly. ''You know the odds are against it.'' *Please, God,* she silently prayed, *I can't be pregnant again. If I am, I'll never be able to leave Jake. Letting him go is already difficult enough.*

''Yeah, I know, but if we stay married, we could have more kids. Wouldn't you like to give Sugar Baby some brothers and sisters?''

''One child is quite enough…''

''By the way, who's taking care of our girl?'' Jake asked.

''Sheila's with her.''

''Ah, so my sister-in-law is the one who informed you where you could find me tonight.''

Donna stared directly at Jake, suddenly realizing just why he'd gone to see Caleb and told his brother about his plans to get drunk and pick up a willing woman. ''You wanted me to know! You knew I'd come after you! Why you—'' Donna spluttered. ''You egotistical—'' she balled her hands into tight fists, gritted her teeth and screeched "—maniacal bastard, you!"

Jake steered the Jeep off the road, onto the edge of an open field. He killed the motor, unsnapped his safety belt and Donna's, then reached over and pulled her into his arms. Before she could say another word, he kissed her.

She broke the kiss, shoved him away and glared at him. Jake leaned back against the driver's side door, crossed his muscular arms over his broad chest and grinned. She wanted to slap that self-assured smile off his face, but she didn't. She sat there fuming, uncertain what to say or do next. Jake had a way of using even her own fury against her.

"I told you that we always get in trouble when we talk," he said. "We both wind up saying things we can't take back. So let's make a pact, at least for tonight." He held out his hand.

She stared suspiciously at his outstretched hand. "What sort of pact?"

"Just for the rest of the night, we aren't going to discuss our marriage—the pros and cons—why we should or shouldn't stay married. No more arguing. About anything."

"We can't put off—"

He pressed his right index finger over her lips. "Yes, we can. For one night. You'd like to spend the night in my arms, wouldn't you, sugar? Admit it to yourself, if not to me. And God knows, I want one more night in your bed."

One more night could lead to a lifetime of sweet loving nights, he told himself. Sooner or later, Donna would stop loving her dead husband and open up her heart to the possibility of sharing her life with another man. He intended to be that man. He could make Donna happy, if she'd give him half a chance.

Donna knew she could lie to Jake, but she wouldn't. No

more lies. Not now or in the future. She could not allow herself to love him, but she could be honest with him. Tomorrow, she would tell him why they couldn't stay married.

"You're right," she told him. "I would like to spend the night in your arms."

Before dawn, Jake woke her. She opened her eyes drowsily and smiled at him, then opened her arms and welcomed him into her embrace and into her body. They made love slowly, maddeningly, driving each other to the breaking point, then retreated to form a new attack. When release claimed them, they absorbed every ounce of satisfaction and then fell asleep again, to be awakened hours later by Louisa's insistent cries.

Jake brought his hungry daughter to her mother's waiting arms. He lay beside his wife and watched their little girl take nourishment from Donna's body. He knew in that one beautiful, perfect moment that he was in love with Donna. He loved her in a way he had never loved anyone. How long he had loved her, he didn't know. It didn't really matter—he knew it now.

Jake noticed the morning sunshine pouring in through the French doors that led to the balcony. Last night's storm had passed and left the earth renewed, fresh and alive. Had his own personal storm passed? Was Donna ready to admit that they belonged together, that even if she didn't love him, she cared for him and wanted him? He was willing to take whatever she offered. He could wait for her to put the past to rest. He would be patient and understanding and allow her the time she needed to learn to love him. He had to find a way to make her understand that they belonged together—now and for the rest of their lives. She was his. And he was never going to let her go.

When Louisa finished nursing, Jake lifted his daughter

into his arms and held her up for inspection. She wriggled and cooed and smiled at her daddy. "Look at her," Jake said. "She's getting so big."

"Dr. Nelson says that she's in the ninety-fifth percentile in height and weight for her age, which means she'll probably be a tall, big woman," Donna told him.

"Takes after her old man."

Jake kissed Louisa's cheeks. She squealed. He and Donna laughed. The moment was so perfect, so pure and sweet and right. A man, his wife and child sharing a morning of family togetherness.

"I want you and Sugar Baby to come out to the ranch today," Jake said. "I want to show you around. The house needs a lot of work, but all you have to do is tell me what you want to do to it and I'll—"

"Jake…" Donna grasped his arm.

He laid Louisa across his chest, her head on his shoulder. "Yeah?"

How was she going to tell him? Was there any way to let him down easy? She should have known that he would assume their marriage was secure and their futures were united.

"I'll bring Louisa out to the ranch…today, if that's what you want." Donna forced herself to look directly into his dark eyes—eyes that were filled with love and happiness. "But there's no need for me to make suggestions about renovating the house."

"Don't tell me that you want to leave all that to me." Jake grinned, then nuzzled Louisa's neck. "Your mama's got to know that I don't know the first thing about turning an old farmhouse into a suitable home for you and her."

Oh, God, help me! Donna closed her eyes, shutting out the sight of Jake's smiling face, of their daughter lying contentedly on his chest. Be strong, she told herself. End things now. Before it hurts too much.

"Jake, I'm not ever going to live on the ranch with you," she blurted as she opened her eyes and looked at him. "Despite what happened last night, nothing has changed. I still plan to get a divorce."

# Eleven

The smile vanished from Jake's face. He spread his big hand out over Louisa's back in a possessive gesture. He'd been fooling himself believing Donna had realized they belonged together for the long haul. Despite everything they shared—including their daughter—she was still damned and determined to end their marriage.

"I'm not going to let you do this," Jake said in a calm, deep voice that concealed the anger raging inside him. "You know as well as I do that we can make a go of this marriage. We've got so much going for us. Why can't you see it?"

"I do see it," she admitted. "But it doesn't matter, I can't."

"Can't stop loving Edward Fields!" What other reason could there be? Jake wondered. It was the only explanation that made any sense.

Donna slipped out of bed, turned her back on Jake and

searched in her closet for a lightweight robe. *You have to tell him the truth! He has a right to know the real reason you intend to end this marriage. You can't let him go on torturing himself with the belief that you're still in love with Edward.*

She walked out of the closet just as Jake laid Louisa in the middle of the bed. He got up, jerked on his discarded jeans and zipped them, but left the button undone.

When he walked toward her, she held up her hands in a keep-away warning gesture. He stopped dead-still. "I'm willing to give you all the time you need to get over your first husband," Jake said. "Sooner or later, you'll have to let go of him. And when you do, I'll be here waiting for you."

"Oh, Jake." Slumping her shoulders as the weight of the world descended upon her, Donna lowered her head and bit down on her lip to keep herself from crying. "I wish it were that simple."

"But it is that simple. I'm not asking you to love me. Not now. I'm willing to take what you can give me and hope that someday you'll learn to love me." He took a tentative step toward her, but halted when she backed away from him.

That was what she feared the most—falling in love with Jake. She cleared her throat, trying to dislodge the emotional lump restricting her speech. "I'm not still in love with Edward."

"You're not?" Jake's lips formed a fragile smile.

"No, I'm not." Donna's heartbeat pounded in her ears. "Of course, a part of me will always love Edward. He was my first love, my husband, my very life, but I'm not still in love with him. I had to force myself to let go of him several years ago."

"Then what's the problem?" Jake's body leaned toward

hers, like a plant seeking nourishment from the sun. "If you don't love him, then don't you think you could learn to love me? I know I'm a little rough around the edges, but you could polish those edges. I'd be putty in your hands."

"Don't do this, Jake. Don't make it any more difficult than it already is. Please, try to understand why I can't stay married to you."

"That's the problem, sugar, I don't understand." His gaze narrowed, focusing directly on her face. "Maybe you'd better explain it to me."

Louisa gurgled and then whimpered. Donna ran to the bed and lifted her child into her arms. "You can see Louisa whenever you want, and spend as much time with her as you'd like. I'll never try to keep her away from you. I promise."

"I appreciate that, but we weren't talking about my rights as Louisa's father. We were discussing our marriage and the reason you're determined to end it."

"I can never love you. Never!"

Jake felt as if he'd been hit in the head with a sledge-hammer.

"I see. Well, that's pretty plain. You've made it clear all along that I wasn't good enough for you. Stupid me, I thought you felt differently now."

"It isn't you," she told him. "It's me."

"Right, it's you. You've got a master's degree, a ton of money and a social position you inherited from your parents. A lady like you can't spend her life married to a worthless cowpoke like me. What on earth would your friends think? They'd probably ban you from the country club!"

Jake hurriedly put on his wrinkled shirt, then stuffed his feet into his socks and pulled on his boots. He stomped out of the room, while Donna stood there holding Louisa. The minute she realized he was leaving, she ran after him.

When she reached the head of the staircase, she called to him. "Jake, please, wait!"

He paused in the middle of the staircase, but didn't turn to face her. "Why should I wait?"

"You're wrong about the way I feel," she said. "I know my so-called friends thought I'd married beneath me. But I never felt that way about you. I've discovered what a wonderful man you are. You're intelligent and loyal and loving and—"

Abruptly Jake turned toward her. "What are you trying to tell me?"

Donna took one hesitant step at a time, descending the stairs slowly, until she paused at Jake's side, halfway down. She petted a whimpering Louisa. "I was deeply in love with Edward." She cringed when she noticed the pained look on Jake's face. "When I love, I love completely." She cleared her throat and tried again. "Edward's death nearly destroyed me. I've never known such agony."

"I don't need to hear this!" Jake turned from her and took the steps two at a time.

"Wait, Jake." Donna hurried to the bottom of the stairs. "I had an emotional breakdown about three months after Edward died. I couldn't sleep. I couldn't eat. I couldn't function well enough to do the most menial tasks. One day, at the college, I collapsed. My uncle Duncan talked me into getting psychiatric help. It took over a year of therapy before I recovered enough to resume my normal life."

Jake stood there, silent and unmoving, his gaze riveted to her tear-glazed eyes.

When he made no comment, she continued. "I made myself a promise once I was well and in control of my life again."

"What sort of promise?" Jake asked.

"I promised myself that I'd never fall in love again."
Donna repeatedly stroked Louisa's back. "That I'd never
give another man that much control over my life—over my
sanity. Don't you see, Jake, I will never allow myself to
fall in love with you."

Jake crumbled before her very eyes—the effect of her
admission. But by the time she moved toward him, one
hand reaching out, he had put himself back together and
his expression had turned to stone. He balled his big hands
into clenched fists.

"You deserve a woman who can love you with all her
heart and soul," Donna said, her voice laced with tears. "I
can never be that woman."

He just stared at her, his eyes cold and hard, his expression emotionless. He turned, opened the front door and
walked out onto the porch, then slammed the door behind
him.

Louisa cried out as if she knew her father was leaving
them. Cuddling her daughter close, Donna grasped the
doorknob and opened the door just in time to see Jake back
his Jeep out of the driveway.

"Jake!" she called. "Don't leave. Please, don't leave
this way."

He revved the Jeep's motor, backed out onto the street
and sped away from the house. Donna slumped down on
the front steps and, cradling Louisa in her arms, wept in a
way she hadn't cried since the day Edward died.

Donna had spent the past month in abject misery, every
day without Jake worse than the day before. Oh, he called
every morning to check on Louisa and stopped by every
night to spend time with her, but not once had he inquired
about anything personal concerning Donna. He hadn't so

much as asked her how she was doing. And when he was in her presence, he looked right through her, as if she didn't exist.

She had thought losing Edward was the worst thing that could ever happen to her—she'd been wrong. Losing Jake, through her own stupidity, was far worse. It had taken her three weeks to realize that she had made the biggest mistake of her life by rejecting Jake's offer to try to make their marriage work. She had thought that by refusing to love him, by ending their marriage, she could protect herself from ever being hurt again. What she hadn't realized at the time was that it was too late. She was already in love with Jake. She'd been trying so hard not to love him that she hadn't recognized the signs.

From the second he'd walked out the front door and left her crying on the steps, she hadn't had one content moment. All she could think about, morning, noon and night was Jake. The way he walked and talked and laughed. The way he made her feel when he looked at her, when he touched her, when he made love to her. The happiness she felt whenever she watched him with Louisa and the joy she'd experienced lying secure and sated in his arms.

She missed Jake as much as she had missed Edward during those first horrendous days after his death. And even though Louisa saw her daddy daily, she missed him, too. Donna knew instinctively that her baby girl felt the loss of her father's presence during the night when he often changed her diaper and rocked her back to sleep. And in the mornings when he took her downstairs and talked to her while she sat in her carrier and watched him fix breakfast. And right before bedtime, when he sang "You Are My Sunshine" to her.

Donna wanted him back—in her arms, in her bed, in her life. Permanently. But it was too late. Jake had already started divorce proceedings and whenever she tried to talk to him about anything the least bit personal, he cut her off short. The warm, loving man who had asked her, *Don't you think you could learn to love me?* had changed into a cold, distant stranger who wouldn't even look at her.

Jake recognized Donna's Corvette parked in front of the farmhouse. What the hell was she doing here? He glanced from the car to the porch. There she sat in the swing, Louisa on her lap. His gaze drifted downward to porch floor beside the swing. Two suitcases rested against the wall. A tight knot of apprehension formed in the pit of his stomach. Just what was going on? Why was Donna here and why had she brought suitcases with her?

The minute she saw him, she jumped up from the swing and, with Louisa in her arms, came running toward him. He stopped and waited for her to come to him. She hesitated a couple of feet away from him, then she smiled and Jake's whole body tensed painfully.

"Hello, Jake," she said.

"What are you doing here?" How many times had he dreamed that Donna would come to him, here at the ranch, and bring his daughter to him? How many restless nights had he envisioned her in his house, in his bed, in his arms?

"Louisa misses you terribly," Donna said, her eyes bright with hope as she gazed at Jake. "And I miss you, too. Terribly."

Jake shifted his booted feet, kicking up a small cloud of dust. "So Louisa misses me and you brought her out for a visit?" He glanced down at the suitcases. "You going to leave her with me for a few days?"

"Not exactly."

"Then what are you doing here? And why the suitcases?"

"We… Louisa and I have come to stay," Donna said bravely.

Jake shook his head to dislodge the cobwebs in his brain. He thought Donna had said that she and Louisa had come to stay. "What did you say?"

"Louisa and I are moving out here to live with you on the ranch."

"I'm not amused with your little joke." Jake walked past Donna and stepped up on the porch.

"Wait a minute," she called after him. "This is no joke!" She followed him up onto the porch. "I don't want a divorce. I want us to stay married."

He skewered her with his deadly cold glare. "Is that so? Just what changed your mind? Are you pregnant again?"

"What?" she gasped.

"I can't think of any other reason you'd want to stay married to me. After all, you don't love me and never will, so why subject yourself to the torture of being married to me unless—"

"Jake Bishop, I could strangle you! You stupid—" She spluttered, then took a deep breath and stomped her foot. Louisa whimpered. "It's all right, Sugar Baby," Donna said. "Your father is just being a stubborn, pigheaded fool."

"Well, are you or are you not pregnant?" he asked.

"No, I'm not pregnant."

"Then why are you here?"

"Because I don't want a divorce. I want us to stay married and give Louisa two loving parents in one home." She glanced around at the peeling paint on the old weathered farmhouse. "This home. After I make this place a home with a little renovation."

She surveyed her husband from the top of his sweat-stained Stetson to the tips of his dirty boots. He was a hot, sweaty, filthy man—her man. And she loved him. Loved his smile. Loved his laugh. Loved his big, hard body. And loved him for being a caring father and a passionate lover.

Rooting at Donna's breast, Louisa cried loudly. "Shh-hh, it's all right. Mama's going to feed you." She looked at Jake. "I'd rather not nurse her out here on the porch, just in case any of the ranch hands happen by."

"Take her inside," Jake said. "While you're nursing her, I'll take care of a few business calls before I take a shower. Then we'll get to the bottom of your little change of heart."

"All right." She smiled triumphantly.

When he opened the door for her, she carried Louisa inside the house and followed Jake through the small, dreary foyer and into the living room. She couldn't stop herself from groaning after her first glimpse. It was obvious the place hadn't been redecorated in a long time, probably not in at least thirty years. And the furniture looked as if it had been purchased in the fifties.

"The whole house looks this bad," Jake said. "Some of the rooms are even worse."

"Paint and wallpaper can do wonders," Donna said. "And the floors need refinishing and—"

"Don't make any plans to start remodeling. You won't be staying long enough to change the sheets on my bed!" He left her alone in the dismal living room.

Her gaze followed his departure, watching him go up the stairs and disappear into one of the many rooms. She took the diaper bag from her shoulder, removed a vinyl pad and a diaper and laid her daughter down on the threadbare sofa.

"Your daddy isn't going to make this easy for me."

Donna quickly changed Louisa's diaper, then glanced around in search of a rocker. There wasn't one, so she sat in the armchair that matched the floral sofa, opened her blouse and bra and put Louisa to her breast. She rocked back and forth and crooned the melody of "You Are My Sunshine" to her child.

"He's not going to send us away," Donna said. "This is home now, Sugar Baby, be it ever so humble. And whether your daddy likes it or not, I'm going to use my own money to remodel this shack and turn it into a livable house. And if his macho pride is offended, then that's just too bad."

Donna continued telling Louisa about her plans while the child nursed and dozed off to sleep. When Louisa released Donna's nipple, she stood and carried Louisa upstairs in search of a bed. She entered the room Jake had gone into and found a bedroom with an old iron bedstead. The sheets were rumpled, but they looked clean. She eased Louisa down in the middle of the bed and rearranged the quilt, spread and pillows to form a cocoon around her sleeping child.

The adjoining bathroom door stood ajar. The sound of running water told Donna that Jake was still in the shower. Acting purely on instinct and a primeval need to recapture and hold her man, Donna undressed, laid her clothes on a rickety wooden chair Jake was using as a nightstand and tiptoed into the bathroom. She could make out Jake's silhouette through the translucent white shower curtain. Her body tightened and released with anticipation. She eased back the curtain and stepped into the old claw-footed tub.

Jake jerked around and glared at her. "What the hell do you think you're doing?"

Donna slid her arms around his neck and rubbed her breasts against his wet, hairy chest. He sucked in a deep breath.

"I'm going to show my husband how much I love him." Standing on tiptoe, she tried to kiss him.

Jake grabbed her shoulders and shoved her away from him. When she lost her balance, he reached out, grasped her around the waist and damned himself for a fool when his sex sprung to life against her mound.

"Don't do this to me," he told her. "Unless you mean it, don't pretend you love me."

She slipped her arms around his waist and laid her head on his chest. The spray of water spewed out over their naked bodies. "Once you were gone, I realized that despite my best efforts to not fall in love with you, I did. I think I probably fell in love with you that first weekend we spent together in New Mexico."

Tremors racked Jake's body. He clasped her face in his hands and forced her to look at him. "I probably fell in love with you then, too, sugar, but I didn't realize that I loved you until the night you came after me at the Pale Rider."

"Can you ever forgive me for—"

He silenced her with a kiss—a kiss that told her he had missed her as much as she had missed him. They devoured each other like hungry animals, wild with their need.

"I don't have any condoms," he said, his voice a ragged whisper.

"It's all right." She licked his neck. "I don't mind if I get pregnant again. I want us to have more children."

"Ah, sugar!"

He lifted her up and braced her against the wall, then drove into her, sending his shaft deep into her hot, wet depths. She clung to him as he maneuvered her hips in a rhythmic beat that quickly brought them both to earth-shattering climaxes. While tingling ashes from the sensual fire they'd created spread a sated warmth through their bodies, Jake withdrew and lowered her to her feet. They bathed each other with slow, tender strokes that soon returned them to heated passion. Jake helped her out of the tub, then briskly dried her with a large towel.

When he picked her up and headed out the door, she said, "Sugar Baby's asleep in your bed."

With Donna in his arms, he turned back into the bathroom, then rested her hips on the sink and brought her legs up and around his waist. She leaned her head back against the mirror over the sink and clasped Jake tightly, urging him to action.

An hour later Jake sat at the scuffed kitchen table, mumbling gibberish to Louisa, while Donna scrambled eggs and prepared buttered toast for their supper.

"I want you to fix this place up," Jake said. "Do anything you want to do. Tear out walls, bring in a contractor. Whatever it takes for you to be happy here."

Donna spooned the eggs onto two plates that already held the toast, picked up the plates and placed them on the table. Coming up behind Jake, she leaned over, curled her arms around him and hugged him fiercely.

"I'm already happy here," she said. "I'm happy because Louisa and I are with you. It doesn't matter where we are as long as we're together."

Jake pulled her around and down onto his lap. "Did I tell you how much I love you, Mrs. Bishop?"

"You told me and showed me." She kissed him on both cheeks. "Jake, I know you can't afford to renovate this place right now, and although I would be glad to use my own money, if it would bother you, then I can wait to fix up this place. I don't need a fine house or beautiful furniture. All I need—all I'll ever need is you!"

Jake kissed her, then said, "There's something I need to tell you about the state of my finances."

"It's all right. Really it is. I know you don't have any

money and that you had to borrow from Caleb to buy this ranch and—''

He shook her gently to gain her attention and silence her. ''I didn't borrow a dime from Caleb or anybody else to buy this place. I paid cash for this ranch. I own it free and clear.''

''But I don't understand, how could you—''

''I'm not penniless,'' he said. ''At last count, my financial advisor estimated my net worth at somewhere in the neighborhood of seven million dollars. Do you think that'll be enough to renovate this old house?''

Donna stared at him, her mouth agape. ''Seven million dollars?''

''Yeah, give or take a few thousand.''

''I don't have nearly that much money.''

''You don't?'' Jake teased.

''I have about a half a million in assets, but—'' She swatted his shoulders and chest. ''Jake Bishop, you let me think you didn't have a dime to your name. How could you—''

''I never told you that I was broke, you just assumed that I was.''

''What were you doing working as a ranch hand out in New Mexico, if you were a millionaire?'' she asked.

''I was learning the quarter horse business before I came back to Tennessee and bought my own ranch.''

Suddenly Donna burst into laughter. She snuggled up against Jake and said, ''You do realize that you're probably richer than any of my snooty friends, don't you?''

''So, what would you like for me to do, buy the country club and toss them out on their ears?'' Jake slid his hand inside her robe and fondled her breast.

''We aren't going to have time to bother with that bunch.'' Donna eased her hand down inside his robe and spread her hands possessively across his chest. "We're going to be too busy on our ranch. Making love and making babies."

"Ah, sugar, I like the way you plan on keeping me busy."

*   *   *   *   *

*Look for Beverly Barton's next
book from Intimate Moments!
Coming in July 1999,* KEEPING ANNIE SAFE,
*a new book in her ongoing series,*
THE PROTECTORS—*only from
Silhouette Intimate Moments!*

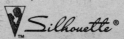

# CATCH THE BOUQUET!

These delightful stories of love and passion, by three of the romance world's bestselling authors, will make you look back on your own wedding with a smile—or give you some ideas for a future one!

# THE MAN SHE MARRIED

by

# ANN MAJOR

# EMMA DARCY

# ANNETTE BROADRICK

*Available at your favorite retail outlet.*

PSBR599

*Silhouette* ®SPECIAL EDITION®

presents **THE BRIDAL CIRCLE**, a brand-new
miniseries honoring friendship, family and love...

### THE BRIDAL CIRCLE

by

# Andrea Edwards

**They dreamed of marrying and leaving their
small town behind—but soon discovered there's
no place like home for true love!**

### IF I ONLY HAD A...HUSBAND (May '99)

Penny Donnelly had tried desperately to forget charming
millionaire Brad Corrigan. But her heart had a memory—and a
will—of its own. And Penny's heart was set on Brad becoming
her husband....

### SECRET AGENT GROOM (August '99)

When shy-but-sexy Heather Mahoney bumbles onto secret agent
Alex Waterstone's undercover mission, the only way to protect the
innocent beauty is to claim her as his lady love. Will Heather
carry out her own secret agenda and claim Alex as her groom?

### PREGNANT & PRACTICALLY MARRIED
### (November '99)

Pregnant Karin Spencer had suddenly lost her memory and
*gained* a pretend fiancé. Though their match was make-believe,
Jed McCarron was her dream man. Could this bronco-bustin'
cowboy give up his rodeo days for family ways?

*Available at your favorite retail outlet.*

*Silhouette* ®

Look us up on-line at: http://www.romance.net          SSETBC

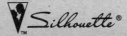

# COMING NEXT MONTH